LOVE'S Redemption

BRENDA DAVIS

ISBN 979-8-88644-005-8 (Paperback)
ISBN 979-8-88644-006-5 (Digital)

Copyright © 2022 Brenda Davis
All rights reserved
First Edition

All rights reserved. No part of this publication may be reproduced, distributed, or transmitted in any form or by any means, including photocopying, recording, or other electronic or mechanical methods without the prior written permission of the publisher. For permission requests, solicit the publisher via the address below.

Covenant Books
11661 Hwy 707
Murrells Inlet, SC 29576
www.covenantbooks.com

And the greatest of these is love.

Chapter 1

Nancy Blackwell arrived in Crestmont, Texas, on a hot July day. Her sister, Susan Montgomery, was meeting her and her daughter, Sarah, at the bus station.

Sarah, her five-year-old daughter, spoke up, "I want my pink princess backpack, Mommy!"

Reaching back into the seat they had just vacated, Nancy picked up the backpack. "I've got it, princess. Now let's get off this bus and see if we can find Aunt Susan."

As they stepped out of the bus, the hot, humid air hit her in the face, causing her to instantly break out in a sweat. She could feel the beads of sweat running under her blouse and down her back.

"Let's hope that Aunt Susan hasn't forgotten us—it's way too hot to be standing in this sun."

"I'm thirsty," Sarah whined.

"If Aunt Susan isn't here, we'll go inside and get a soda. But first we need to make sure Aunt Susan isn't waiting for us. We don't want to miss her."

Glancing around the parking lot, she saw people who had come on the same bus retrieving their luggage. She knew she needed to get hers and Sarah's, but she wanted to find her sister first. She didn't want to be lugging her heavy suitcases around looking for her.

Susan had said she was driving a small blue compact car. She saw one just pulling in at the far end of the parking lot. Sighing, she wiped the sweat from her forehead, tousling her bangs. In this heat, she was glad she had pulled her medium-length blond hair up into a ponytail on the back of her head. She knew the Texas heat would be murder even before she ever left Oklahoma. That's why she had decided the ponytail would serve the purpose.

Nancy turned as she heard her name being called. She smiled as she saw her sister rushing toward them. Susan hadn't changed in the two years since she had seen her. Susan was younger than her by three years. Even though Nancy was only twenty-eight, sometimes she felt decades older than her lively sister.

"Nancy, oh, I'm so glad you are both here! It's been a long time," Susan said as she reached out and hugged Nancy.

Sarah jumped up and down. "Auntie Susan! Auntie Susan!"

"Hi, princess!" Susan said as she reached down and pulled Sarah up into a gigantic hug, swinging her around. "Auntie Susan has been waiting and waiting for you to come!"

Sarah squealed in delight at being swung around, "I've been waiting since thirteen o'clock for you!"

Susan laughed as she heard Sarah's favorite saying about time. "I've been waiting for you since fourteen o'clock…or two years anyway." She glanced up at Nancy.

"I'm sorry I didn't come sooner, but since Joe's death, my life's just been turned upside down," Nancy said, glancing away from Susan, trying to blot out the memories.

"I know it's been hard for you, but you're here with me now, and I'm praying that God will work things out for you," Susan said, knowing that her sister hadn't depended on God for a long time.

Nancy got a frown on her face and said, "Don't talk to me about God. When I really needed him, he wasn't there."

"God was there when Sarah was born. If it hadn't been for God, she would've died," Susan reminded her.

Nancy looked down at her five-year-old daughter, remembering when she was born. But the vision of her husband and their trouble almost blotted out the blessings of Sarah's birth.

"The doctors said if Sarah lived, she would never walk. Look at her now, she's not just walking, but she's running! You can't deny that God didn't do something," Susan reminded Nancy.

Nancy knew in her heart that what Susan was saying was true, but after all the problems in her life, all of the things she had gone through, it made her unwilling to admit to the goodness of God.

"Susan, I just don't want to talk about it right now, maybe later, but not right now. I'm tired, and I know Sarah is. Besides it's hot, and I'd really like to take a long shower."

Sarah reached into the small pink princess purse that she had clutched in her hands the whole way from Oklahoma, pulling out a small book. "Lookie, Aunty Susan, Mamaw gave me this pretty book…it's a Bible!" In her small hand, she held a tiny pink Bible with her name in gold at the bottom.

Nancy quickly snatched the book from her daughter's hand and threw it across the parking lot in a fit of fury. "Sarah, I told you to leave that book at Mamaw's!"

She couldn't believe that her mother would defy her and give her daughter something she didn't want her to have. As soon as she could, she would call her mother and let her that she didn't appreciate the interference.

Sarah watched as her pretty pink book landed on the pavement and slid a little ways on the concrete. She quickly ran toward the book, crying, "It's my book! Mamaw gave it to me!"

"Sarah, you come back here!" Nancy screamed as she ran after her.

"No! I want my book!" the little girl cried.

Nancy watched as her daughter ran to the pink Bible that lay with its pages fluttering in the wind. The blond hair on her daughter flew every which way as she reached down and picked up her precious book. She turned with a triumphant look at her mother, holding the book high above her head, "I gots it! I gots it!"

Sarah was so proud of her accomplishment that she never noticed the gray sedan that was coming around the corner a little too fast. Nancy watched in horror as the car's front fender struck Sarah a glancing blow, sending her sprawling onto the pavement and her head making a sickening thud as it hit the concrete.

"Sarah!" Nancy screamed as the car slowed only slightly before careening out of the parking lot and pulled out in front of an oncoming traffic. Car horns honked in protest at the offending vehicle.

"Call 911!" Screaming at Susan, Nancy ran toward her daughter, and that was when she noticed a dark-haired man running toward Sarah. When she got beside her daughter, the dark-haired man was already leaning over Sarah.

"Sarah…Sarah!" Nancy screamed over and over as she knelt beside the still body of her little girl.

The man paid no attention to her but continued to check Sarah's vital signs. Nancy started to raise her head, but the man said in a firm voice, "No, don't move her. The ambulance is on its way." In the distance, the wailing of a siren could be heard.

Susan rushed over to them and said, "I called 911—they're sending out an ambulance and the police."

The man responded, "Good, she needs to go to the hospital immediately. I think she has a concussion." He continued to watch Sarah closely, lifting her eyelids and checking her heartbeat. Within just a few moments, the paramedics were beside them.

They worked quickly, gently putting Sarah in a neck brace and placing her on the gurney. The man walked beside the paramedics, speaking, "Her breathing is steady but shallow. I found her already unconscious when I got here."

Nancy watched as if she was looking upon a surreal scene. It couldn't be her little girl they were putting in the ambulance; Sarah was only five years old. Nancy remembered another time when she had almost called for an ambulance, but Joe wouldn't let her. He said he didn't want the doctors poking their noses into family problems.

She had a flashback of Joe saying, "Don't worry about it, Nancy! She'll be fine. Besides, you know doctor's only want your money, they don't care about anything else."

Nancy stood helplessly beside Susan as the paramedics were asking her questions. She answered them, but she couldn't seem to really focus on what was happening.

Suddenly, she felt a hand on her arm. Turning, she saw the dark-haired man. She looked up into his face and saw compassion and something else, something she couldn't identify, but his dark eyes seemed to convey strength.

"Ma'am, your little girl was holding this. Do you want to take it with you so she'll have it at the hospital?"

Looking down, Nancy saw that he was hold the little pink Bible. It was smudged a little from where it had hit the pavement when she had thrown it. It was the last thing that Sarah had held. How could she not accept it? Nancy's heart seemed to sink within her. How could she have been so stupid? She had thrown the pink Bible in a fit of anger, and now her daughter was paying for what she had done.

Nancy reached out and took the Bible, holding it tenderly. "T-thank you. Do you know where they are taking her?"

"Crestmont Medical Center...it's only a few miles from here. Do you have a ride?" the man asked.

"Y-yes, my sister..." her voice trailed off as Susan spoke up.

"I'm her sister, Susan. I just came to pick them up. I'll take her over there."

Nancy was still in a daze, but she remembered she hadn't gotten her and Sarah's luggage. "Wait, I've got to get our suitcases! And didn't you say that the police would be here?"

"Don't worry about them, ma'am. What's your name? I'll get the suitcases and bring them to the hospital. And I'll let the police know where to find you. They'll have to make out a report on what happened." The man was offering his help again.

"Her name's Nancy Blackwell, and here are the baggage claim tickets," Susan answered for her, handing over the tickets to the man.

Susan grabbed Nancy's arm and said, "Come on, you'll want to be at the hospital as soon as possible. I'm sure Sarah will be needing you."

Looking at the man, Nancy stammered, "T-thank you. There are three bags and a small backpack. Sarah will—" Suddenly she stopped and realized that her baby lay in an ambulance headed to an unknown hospital without her. Tears flowed down her cheeks as she turned and hurried to her sister's car, not caring if her bags were brought or not, she just had to get to her baby.

Marc Carter watched as the slim, blond-haired woman got into the small blue car. The woman stirred something within him, something that hadn't been stirred in a long time. Shaking his head, he tried to put the memories of his wife and daughter from his mind.

After retrieving the bags from the terminal, he slipped into the leather seat of his car, turning the key and feeling the rush of the air conditioner as it started to cool the interior. Memories of Melanie, his wife, rushed into his brain again. Memories of her always wanting to turn the air conditioner off and roll the windows down. She wanted to let the wind ruffle her hair. She never did like what she had called fake air.

Pulling the car out of the parking spot, he glanced down at the luggage that filled the bucket seat and noticed the pink backpack, remembering that his daughter, Amber, had loved pink. Amber…his little girl that never got to grow up. Amber and his wife had been hit and killed by a drunk driver while they were shopping.

Seeing the little girl lying still in the parking lot brought back the memories of his wife and daughter. And then seeing the pink Bible and backpack…it was almost too much.

Marc made his way into the parking lot of the hospital, finding his private space among the physicians' section. He pulled in and turned off the motor. For a moment, he sat in the car, his hands clenching and unclenching the steering wheel as he prayed, "Lord, I thought I had gotten over the bitterness from Melanie and Amber's death. I thought I had forgiven the man that was drunk and had run the stop sign. Please, Lord, help me again. I don't want to feel that hatred."

Marc sat in the quietness and felt the almost tangible touch that gave him peace again. Taking a deep sigh of relief, he opened the door and stepped out into the sunshine.

Chapter 2

Nancy rushed into the emergency waiting room moments after the ambulance arrived. The waiting room was crowded with sick people and their loved ones as she hurried toward the receptionist desk.

"I want to see my daughter. She was just brought in by ambulance!" Nancy said, her voice trembling with fear.

The gray-haired woman behind the desk looked at her with sympathy and said, "What's your daughter's name?"

"Sarah Blackwell. She's five years old."

Checking the records, the woman said, "Yes, she was just brought in by ambulance. You can see her in just a few minutes. They're getting her comfortable right now. While you're waiting, could I get some information from you?"

Nancy fumbled in her purse for the information that was needed, thankful that Susan had come in from parking the car and now stood beside her. Susan gave the woman her address and information for contact. Nancy glanced through the window in the door that separated the waiting room from the back and was surprised to see the dark-haired man walk by on the other side.

In just a few moments, they were done, and Nancy was ushered back into the room where Sarah lay covered by a thin sheet. Tears blurred her vision as she hurried toward her tiny daughter. Tears ran down her cheeks as she reached over and gently smoothed back Sarah curly blond hair.

"Oh, honey, Mommy's so sorry for throwing your Bible like I did." She leaned down and brushed her lips across Sarah's cheeks.

Someone cleared their throat and drew her attention. There standing inside the curtained off emergency room was the man that had helped them. In his hands, he held the pink backpack. "I gave your sister the other suitcases, and she's putting them in her car. I hope that was okay?"

"I appreciate all you did for us. I...I'm sorry, I don't even know your name," Nancy stammered.

"It's Marc, Marc Carter," the man said as he set the backpack down beside the wall and walked to the other side of the bed. "How's she doing?"

"I don't know. I haven't seen the doctor. A nurse brought me back here. I wish they'd hurry."

"I'll go see what I can do," Marc said as he strode out of the curtained off room. In a few minutes, he was back, but this time he had on a white jacket on over his black checked shirt. In his hands, he carried a file.

"It looks like they are going to start an IV, and there's a CT scan scheduled. We're just waiting on a room to open up. She'll have to stay overnight in the hospital so we can make sure she's all right," he said, looking up to see the shocked look on Nancy's face.

"You...you're a doctor?" she asked.

He smiled. "Yes, actually I'm a neurosurgeon. I called into the hospital and let them know I was coming into the hospital at the time of your daughter's accident, Mrs. Blackwell."

"I'd rather you'd just call me Nancy, Dr. Carter."

"All right, Nancy. And this pretty little girl's name is Sarah?" Marc reached over and ran a finger down Sarah's cheek. He couldn't help it. She reminded him so much of Amber.

"Yes, and she's five years old," Nancy said, holding onto her daughter's tiny hand and rubbing her thumb over her fingers.

"Beautiful name. It's a Bible name. Speaking of the Bible, where is that pink Bible that she had?"

Nancy reached down to the floor and lifted up her purse. She opened it up and pulled out the small Bible. "It's right here." She smoothed down the slightly bent corner where it had landed on the concrete when she had thrown it. She lifted Sarah's hand and laid it down, resting her hand back on top of it. "It seems as if this book and my reaction to it caused my daughter all this trouble." Tears began to well up again in Nancy's eyes.

"It can get you out of a lot of trouble too," Marc said. "And right now, Sarah needs all the help she can get. It's the best book she could have."

"Her grandmother gave it to her before we left. I...I didn't even know she had it."

Marc looked at Nancy and saw something flit across her face. Almost as if she wanted to blame this all on the Bible that lay on the white sheet.

"Dr. Carter, Dr. Carter, 7123." A voice came over the intercom.

"Excuse me. I need to answer a call." Marc turned and walked from the room. He walked over to the desk where a young nurse sat. "Mary, they just paged me. Can you hand me the phone?"

The nurse grinned. "Sure, Dr. Carter!" She reached across the desk and handed the phone to Marc but frowned when he turned away from her. She had been trying for almost three months to get this good-looking doctor to notice her but without success. Giving a sigh, she went back to her paperwork but listened to the doctor's deep voice as he spoke on the phone about the new patient that had just come in by ambulance.

Hanging up the phone, he said, "Thanks, Mary. Could you get an orderly to move the patient in trauma room 4 up to radiology for a CT scan?"

"The little girl that just came in by ambulance? Sad, isn't it? She's so pretty," Mary said as she paged one of the orderlies.

Marc nodded, then walked back into the room where Nancy and Sarah were. He wanted to check Sarah over once more before the orderly came. Lifting her eyelids one at a time, he was pleased to see them respond to light. Her pulse seemed normal, and her breathing was good, but he didn't like the fact that she was still unconscious.

"Is she going to be okay, Doctor?" Nancy asked anxiously.

"We'll do all we can for her, but we need to find out if everything is okay inside her head. She hit the pavement pretty hard. That's why there's a large knot right here on the back of her head. But there doesn't seem to be anything major other than that. That's why I want to do a CT scan, just to make sure." Marc hesitated. He was puzzled over a few things but didn't want to alarm Nancy. He'd just wait and see what the scan showed before calling for any further testing.

The orderly appeared at the door and prepared to take Sarah up to Radiology. Marc spoke to Nancy, "She'll be gone about a half hour to an hour. Why don't you and your sister go to the cafeteria and grab something to drink or, better yet, something to eat. It's probably been a while since you've eaten."

"I don't know if I could eat anything right now."

"You won't do Sarah any good by getting sick yourself. Go on and at least get something to drink. When she's back, I'll send someone to get you."

Nancy still wasn't sure, but she was thirsty and did need something to drink. She needed to take something for the headache that she had gotten as soon as she had stepped from the bus into the hot sun. Nodding, Nancy moved toward the waiting room where she found Susan anxious to hear about Sarah.

"Tell me about Sarah. Is everything going to be okay? What did Dr. Carter say? Is he going to be Sarah's doctor?" Susan asked in a rush.

Nancy nodded and then told her about Sarah and the CT scan as they both headed toward the cafeteria. Nancy still couldn't bring herself to eat anything, so she just got something to drink. Susan got a muffin and some coffee, and they both went into the dining room and sat at a nearby table.

Nancy waited until they sat down to ask Susan about the man that had helped them and was obviously the doctor in charge of Sarah.

"You knew that the man that was helping Sarah was a doctor? Why didn't you tell me?" Nancy said as she took two aspirin and a gulp of her soda.

"I work here at the hospital in admitting, Nancy. I just didn't even think to tell you about Marc Carter. He is one of the best neurosurgeons in the country. Crestmont Memorial is lucky to get him. If anything is wrong with Sarah, he'll find it."

"He's a neurosurgeon. Why would Sarah need a neurosurgeon?" Nancy was looking at her watch. It seemed like it had been an hour since she had left Sarah's side, but it had only been about fifteen minutes.

"Hopefully, she won't need one. But since she hit her head on the concrete, it's best that she's checked out. By the way, the police were in the waiting room asking for you. I told them who I was and told them all I knew about the accident. I saw the car and noticed the back fender had some damage. They took the report and were going to talk to the doctor too. I have the deputy's card that he left with me. He wants you to call him as soon as you can." Susan reached into her purse and pulled out a card.

Nancy glanced at it and saw that it said Sergeant Todd Stevens, Crestmont Police Department, along with his phone number. She said, "You keep it, Susan. I don't know if I'll even remember where I put it if I take it. My mind just doesn't want to function right now."

"It's all the stress that you've been under, Nancy. My goodness, with all the things that happened, I don't know how you've been able to stand up under the pressure."

"I've had too. Sarah needed me—she still does. I won't let her down, Susan. She's all I've got."

Susan reached over and placed her hand on top of Nancy's laying on the table and gave her a squeeze. "Not anymore, you've got me...and don't forget you've still got God."

Nancy gave her a tight smile but said nothing. She didn't feel like getting into another argument with Susan over God. And she didn't want to say anything bad about God either. Her little girl lay on a bed somewhere in this hospital, and she couldn't help but let a little prayer go up from her heart, "Please, God...please. If not for me, then please for my princess?"

Chapter 3

It wasn't long before Sarah was brought back to the emergency room, and Marc was reviewing the test results, but the only thing that showed up in the tests was a small dark spot where her head had struck the pavement. However, what had Marc worried was she was still unconscious. This was the reason he was going to keep Sarah in the hospital overnight. If the little girl was still unconscious in the morning, he would order a series of tests to be run.

Knowing Nancy would want to be with her daughter, he made his way to the dining room of the hospital. Looking over in the corner of the nearly empty room, Marc saw Nancy sitting with her sister.

She looked up and saw Marc in the doorway. Standing up quickly, she hurried over to the tall doctor.

"Is she back? What did you find out?" Nancy said.

"She just got back to the ER. The test results didn't seem to show any serious damage," Marc countered.

"Is she awake yet?" Nancy asked hopefully.

"No, no, she hasn't come awake yet. That is what is puzzling. The tests showed a small dark spot on her brain, most likely caused when her head hit the concrete. It looks like a bruise that will heal in time."

Susan, who was standing beside Nancy, said, "Surely there's a reason for her being out so long."

"I agree. There has to be a reason, but sometimes a patient will come out of it, and everything will be all right. Other times, more tests are needed," Marc responded.

"I understand," Nancy said. "And if she wakes up tonight or tomorrow, then we can go home, right?"

"We are going to admit her for observation tonight. If she doesn't wake up by tomorrow morning, I want to run more tests and see if there is something we've missed," Marc said.

As they all three walked back toward the emergency room, he told both Nancy and Susan everything that he knew about Sarah's condition. When they arrive back in the room, the curtains had been pulled, and Sarah lay upon the gurney. The records were at the foot of the bed, and her pink Bible was still lying beside her, tucked securely under her little arm.

Marc picked up the records and reread them, making sure he didn't miss anything. A slight frown marred his smooth tanned complexion. Nancy picked up on his reaction almost immediately.

"What is it? Have you found something else?" she asked anxiously.

"No…I don't see anything else." Closing the file, he said, "We can continue to hope and pray that by tomorrow, this pretty little girl wakes up and will be able to go home."

He walked around to the side of Sarah's bed and tucked a stray blond curl behind her ear, letting his fingers twirl the curl a little before tucking it in. He knew exactly what Nancy was feeling. He remembered standing beside Amber as she lay on a hospital gurney just like this one. He had only had a few moments beside his baby, not wanting to admit that she was gone, just like his wife. Closing his eyes for just a moment, he again sent up a prayer. God was the only reason he had been able to continue to live and work. As time passed, it had gotten a little easier, but at times like this, when it was a child that reminded him of his past, that's when it became hard again.

Nancy watched as the emotions played across the face of the doctor that stood on the other side of the bed. He seemed to be in pain for just a moment before he opened his eyes and met hers.

"Mrs. Blackwell, would you mind if I prayed for Sarah?" Marc asked softly.

Nancy wanted to scream no, but she didn't. She knew that there was a God. She just didn't think he cared about her anymore, but she would do anything, including going back to church, if God would just help her daughter.

"I...I don't mind, Dr. Carter. If you think it will help, go ahead," Nancy said and bowed her head.

Marc reached out and took Sarah's hand and prayed, "Dear Lord, you see this beautiful child that is laying here. She's been hurt in something that wasn't her fault, Lord. We don't know what's wrong, why she doesn't wake up. So we are asking for your help. You are our great physician, and you have created our bodies. Allow Sarah to be healed, Lord. Bring glory to your name. In Jesus's name, we pray. Amen."

Nancy had bowed her head as Marc had prayed, but she stood stiffly, hearing his words but not believing them. She wanted to believe them, but after what she had been through with Joe and God had never stepped in, she didn't put much faith in prayer anymore.

"Thank you, Dr. Carter. I'm sure that Sarah, if she could say something, would appreciate your prayer. She's always gone to church with my mother when I wasn't able to take her."

"So you go to church?" Marc asked.

"I...I used to go, but I haven't been for a while. Let's just say that some things that I really needed help with, God didn't answer."

"Mrs. Blackwell, it's not that God didn't answer your prayers," Marc said.

"What do you mean? You don't know anything about what I went through. I needed God! And when I needed him the most, he wasn't there," Nancy spit out, furious that this man could stand there and speak like that to her.

"God answered your prayers but in his own way, or maybe he was answering your prayers and never had time to finish because you turned away from him. I don't know the mind of God, but I've been through some very bad times in my life. And if it hadn't been for God, I don't know what I would've done," Marc countered.

He continued, "He didn't answer them the way I had wanted him too, but he did answer, and he gave me peace. Who knows, God may have other plans for my life. So I just have to trust in him to do what is best."

Nancy clenched her hands into fists. She wanted to scream and cry and tell this man that he didn't know what he was talking about. He had never gone through what she had gone through. He had never hurt like she had hurt. How could he stand there and tell her about how wonderful God was?

Instead of saying that, Nancy took some deep breaths, and she changed the subject back to her daughter, "Are they going to get Sarah a room soon? I want to be able to stay with her tonight."

"I'll go and check on the status of the room. And I'll make sure they move a cot up there so you can be beside her tonight." Turning, Marc left the room, knowing that he hadn't convinced the beautiful woman standing beside her daughter's bed that God could help her.

Sighing, he walked back to the nurse's station and saw that Mary was still there. "I thought you got off work an hour ago?" he said as he reached for the chart that held the patient's names and rooms if they were going to be admitted.

Mary smiled brightly. "Actually I did, but I figured I'd stick around and see if you'd like to go out and have a cup of coffee with me tonight. Chuck's Place is just around the corner, and he makes a mean cup of java."

"Not that I couldn't use a cup of strong coffee, but it'll be a couple more hours before I'll be able to leave. By that time, I'll be ready to hit the sack. Maybe some other time." Marc sidestepped the nurse's attempt to go out with her.

Mary was frustrated, but she tried to keep it out of her voice as she said, "Sure, Dr. Carter...Marc...maybe some other time." She reached down and picked up her purse and walked out the door.

Marc sighed again. He knew that Mary wanted to go out with him. And she seemed like a really nice person. It's just that he wasn't ready for the dating scene yet. After all, he hadn't been single for a long time...only two years.

Even as these thoughts entered his head, he glanced at the closed curtains to the room where he knew Nancy Blackwell and her daughter were. What was it about Nancy that caused his pulse to beat a little faster whenever he saw her? He had to admit she was a beautiful woman, but he had seen lots of beautiful women. It wasn't her looks as much as her pain that seemed to reach out to him. She had been hurt in the past, badly hurt, but he didn't know how or by whom. Still something about her brown eyes seemed to reach into his soul and bring out a longing to stop her hurting in any way that he could.

    Glancing at the chart, he saw that Sarah's room was ready. The most he could do for now was to make sure that Nancy had a comfortable cot to sleep on tonight while she waited for her daughter to awaken. And he was going to make sure she had whatever she needed while she stayed at the hospital.

Chapter 4

Nancy turned restlessly on the small cot that was provided for her so that she could stay the night in Sarah's room. As she lay there, she could hear the nurses checking on Sarah at regular intervals throughout the night. Even though she didn't get any sleep, she was thankful the nurses were diligent in taking care of Sarah. Every time the nurses came in, they would talk to her daughter, trying to get her to respond to them.

Nancy finally gave up trying to sleep; she squinted at her watch in the darkness, turning it so that the light from the hallway would shine on it. She saw 2:00 a.m., and she couldn't believe it. It seemed like it should at least be six or seven o'clock. She even tapped her watch to make sure it was working, but sure enough she saw the digital display turn over to 2:01 a.m.

Sighing, Nancy got to her feet and moved over to stand beside Sarah. Reaching out, she picked up the little pink Bible that even the nurses had made sure was tuck in securely beside her daughter when they had transferred her to a bed.

Holding it in her hand for a moment, she paused, glancing down at her daughter and then back to the Bible she held in her hand. She closed her eyes, and without thinking, she prayed, "God, I don't understand why you've allowed things to happen to me in my past. I probably haven't done everything that I should have done and that's why you didn't answer my prayers, but Sarah loves to go to church. She believes in you and loves you. Would you please heal her, God? Please? For Sarah's sake?"

She laid the Bible back down beside Sarah and then leaned over and kissed her on her forehead, smoothing back her hair as she whispered, "Sarah, Sarah, it's time to wake up. Come on, honey, wake up for Mommy. We need to go to Auntie Susan's house and help her get our rooms ready."

She waited, hoping and almost praying that Sarah would move, make a sound, or do anything that would show some response, but there was nothing.

"I don't even know why I prayed. God isn't going to do anything for me! That just proves that prayer is just a bunch of empty words!" Frustrated, she turned, quickly planning to return to her cot and lay down. But as she did, she knocked over the water glass that was sitting on the tray table, sending it crashing to the floor.

Suddenly everything seemed to be happening at once! A nurse ran from the nurse's station toward their room and a cry came from Sarah, and Nancy stood there in amazement as her daughter's eyes flew open.

"Sarah!" Nancy said in unbelief.

"Mrs. Blackwell, is everything alright in here?" the nurse asked as she hurried into the room.

"Mommy?" Sarah said.

All of the talking seemed to be happening at once, but when Nancy heard Sarah's sweet little voice, immediately she rushed back to her side.

"Sarah, Mommy's right here."

"Mommy…are we at Auntie Susan's?"

"No, honey, you got hurt, and we had to bring you to the hospital, but everything's going to be okay, and we'll get to go Auntie Susan's house really soon," Nancy said as she gathered Sarah up into a hug.

"Mrs. Blackwell, I'm going to put in a call to Dr. Carter. He left word with us to call him immediately when Sarah woke up," the nurse said as she finished checking Sarah's IV.

"Yes…yes, whatever you think!" Nancy was just thankful to have Sarah awake and responding to her.

It seemed like only minutes later Marc Carter rushed into the room. His hair was still slightly disheveled, and there were dark circles under his eyes, but he had a smile on his face.

"So this little princess decided to wake up, huh?" Marc asked as he stood on one side of Sarah's bed.

"Who are you?" Sarah asked

"That's Dr. Carter, Sarah," Nancy answered for Marc. "He's taking care of you while you're in the hospital."

"Oh, I thought you were an angel," Sarah said.

"Nope, I'm not an angel…first time I've ever been called one." Marc laughed.

"But you look just like the angel that helped me after that car hit me," Sarah said.

Marc stopped laughing and glanced at Nancy. Nancy shook her head, letting him know that she didn't know what Sarah was talking about.

"Did the angel say anything to you, Sarah?" Marc asked quietly.

Sarah closed her eyes for a few moments and then she smiled, "I 'member now. He said that I was going to be fine. And that Mommy would laugh again."

Nancy's eyes filled with tears. She hadn't really laughed in a long, long time. In her life with Joe, there hadn't been much to laugh about. As she thought about it, she realized Sarah probably hadn't heard her laugh much at all. Life was so stressful for them.

"Well, honey, Mommy's happy now! You're awake, and you're going to be fine."

"But, Mommy, the angel told me that you would laugh like you use to before Daddy started—" Sarah didn't finish the sentence.

A blush touched Nancy's face as she thought of what Sarah was about to say. She didn't want the doctor to hear about their sordid life when Joe was alive.

"Daddy's gone, honey. You remember the funeral, right?" Nancy wanted to inject some words that would cause Marc to think that Sarah was speaking of her father's death.

"I 'member, Mommy." As Nancy leaned closer, Sarah reached up a small hand and touched her face. "I told the angel that Daddy didn't make you laugh, but the angel said that it was going to be better for you now, Mommy. I believe the angel 'cause God sent him to me."

Nancy didn't know what to say, so she decided it was best to say nothing at all, but Marc spoke up, "Well, young lady, since you woke us all up in the middle of the night, how about if I check you out and make sure you're doing better? Is that okay with you?"

"Sure…but just be sure you don't check behind my ears," Sarah said.

"Why not?" Marc questioned.

"'Cause Mommy always tells me that I forget to wash there, and it's probably dirty right now."

Marc laughed and brought his stethoscope out, saying, "I promise I won't check behind your ears if you promise me that you'll let me hear your heart."

"Okay," Sarah said as she lay still so that Marc could check her out. He tested her reflexes and her arm and leg movements. Then he tested her eye movements, and everything seemed to check out, except when he shined his light into her eyes. Something didn't seem quite right; her eyes reacted but not as fast as they should have.

Not wanting to worry either of them tonight, Marc put up his equipment and said, "Well, little princess, you're looking very good for two o'clock in the morning." Lowering his voice to almost a whisper, he said to Sarah, "Did you know that most princesses don't look very pretty at two o'clock?"

"Really?" Sarah asked. "I didn't know that." Turning to her mother, she said, "Doctor"—she stopped and turned back to Marc—"What was your name again, Mr. Angel?"

"I'm not an angel, Sarah. My name is Dr. Marc Carter."

Turning back to her mother, she said, "Dr. Marc Angel said I'm a pretty princess even if mostest princesses are not pretty at thirteen o'clock."

Both Marc and Nancy grinned at Sarah's thirteen o'clock. Nancy knew that it was Sarah's favorite time. Whenever she would look at the clock or try to tell time, it was always thirteen o'clock.

Sarah looked at Marc and said, "See, Dr. Marc Angel… Mommy's already smiling! Did you make her smile?"

"No, Princess, I think you did," Marc replied, not bothering to correct the *angel* part of his name.

"Mrs. Blackwell…" Marc started to say.

"I'd just as soon you call me Nancy." Nancy hated the name Blackwell because it only served to reminded her of Joe and the way he had treated her and Sarah. She planned to have her name and Sarah's name changed back to Montgomery as soon as she had the money for a lawyer.

"Nancy," Marc amended. "If this young princess is still doing this good in the morning, then I think she'll be ready to go home."

Nancy and Marc turned at the sound of a nurse entering the room. "I'm sorry, Dr. Carter. I wasn't able to get in here when you did. We had a patient that was very upset and we had to calm him down."

Marc nodded. "That's okay, Marcie. I've checked this little girl out, and she seems to be doing pretty good. I'll be down to the nurse's station in a few minutes to fill out the report. If Sarah gets a good night's sleep tonight, then we'll probably be discharging her in the morning."

The nurse grinned at Sarah. "Well, it looks like when you wake up. You really know how to do it!"

"Sure, I do," Sarah said with a questioning frown on her face. "You just open your eyes, and you waked up! Don't you open your eyes when you wake up?"

The nurse laughed. "Well, you've got me there, kiddo! I guess I do. Now let's get you tucked back into bed and all comfy. Then when you wake up, your mom will be able to take you home tomorrow."

"Goody! I want to go to Auntie Susan's house," Sarah said. Turning her head, she looked at her mother. "Mommy, where is my Bible?"

Reaching under the sheet, Nancy retrieved the little pink book. It had slid under the cover when Sarah had started moving around. "It's right here, darling."

"You're not mad at it anymore, are you, Mommy?" Sarah asked, holding the Bible and looking from it to her mother's face.

"No, honey, I'm not mad at it anymore." Nancy was ashamed of the way she had acted at the bus station. She was hoping that Sarah hadn't remembered that part of the day.

"Goody! 'Cause that means that I can keep Mamaw's Bible that she gaved to me. Mamaw told me that Auntie Susan goes to Sunday school. Can I go to Sunday school with Auntie Susan? Will you go with me?"

Nancy didn't want to be discussing church in front of everyone, so instead she said, "Goodness, you have a lot of questions tonight! How about if we just wait and see what happens? First, you need to get to sleep, and then in the morning, we'll call Auntie Susan, and she'll come and pick us up from the hospital and take us to her house. How does that sound?"

Sarah smiled as she snuggled under the cover, holding her Bible close to her chest. "It sounds like fun, Mommy, but Sunday school sounds like it would be funner."

Nancy sighed and shook her head, glancing up at the doctor and nurse standing at the foot of Sarah's bed. "When she gets something in her mind, she never lets go of it."

Marc smiled. "Sounds like a persistent little girl…and a typical one!"

The nurse laughed and said, "Yep, I have two children, a four-year-old and a six-year-old. I can't get anything over on either one of them. If I promised them something, they never let me forget it. They keep me on my toes."

Marc spoke up, "I'll come in tomorrow morning." He stopped and glanced at his watch. "Well, actually, I guess I'll be here again in just a few hours. That way I can check on Sarah once more and then sign the discharge papers."

"All right, I'll call Susan and get her to come and pick us up. She was planning on coming up here in the morning anyway. So it'll be wonderful that we can just go home," Nancy said.

"Did the police find out anything else about who hit Sarah with their car?" Marc asked.

Frowning, Nancy said, "No...at least I don't *think* they know anything else. I've been up here and haven't heard anything."

"I really hope they find that guy. Nobody should ever leave the scene of an accident...and especially when someone hits a child!" Marc's voice sounded tight as he spoke the words, remembering that the drunk driver who had hit and killed his wife and daughter had fled the scene. The police found him later, and he was put behind bars, but it didn't bring his family back.

Moving toward the door, he said, "I'll see both of you later. Try to get a little sleep, it would do you good."

Nancy smiled slightly and said, "Yes, I know. Most princesses aren't pretty at two o'clock in the morning."

"I... I didn't mean..." Marc stammered and felt his neck get hot.

Still smiling, Nancy said, "You'd better go get your report filled out and get some sleep yourself, Doctor!"

Marc realized that she had been teasing him as he headed toward the nurse's station. At first, he was humiliated to think that Nancy might have thought he meant she wasn't pretty, which was far from the truth. But then he wasn't ready to acknowledge any of those feelings just yet. He figured he was just tired and needed to do as she said...go home and get some sleep.

Chapter 5

Susan arrived at the hospital the next morning to find Nancy and Sarah ready to go. Sarah was bouncing up and down on the side of the bed. When she saw her aunt walk in, she jumped off the bed and ran to her.

Excitedly, she said, "Auntie Susan, I'm all better now!"

"Wow, so I see!" Susan said as she knelt down and gave Sarah a hug. "I'm glad you're okay, sweetie. Auntie Susan was worried about you last night, and I prayed that Jesus would heal you."

"He did! He did! And he sent Dr. Angel to make sure I was taken care of real good too." Turning to Nancy, Sarah said, "Didn't he Mommy?"

Nancy had heard the conversation, but she pretended that she hadn't. "Didn't he what, Sarah?"

"Didn't Jesus send Dr. Angel to take care of me?" Sarah repeated.

"Well, I'm not sure that Dr. Carter could be considered an angel, but the doctor has taken really good care of you." Nancy sidestepped the question that Sarah was asking.

Susan stood up and said, "Did you get much sleep last night, Nancy? I know it's not easy sleeping in the hospital and especially on those small cots."

"Well, I can't say it was the most comfortable place to sleep, but it was okay. As I told you on the phone this morning, Sarah woke up about two o'clock. The nurses called Dr. Carter immediately, and he came back to the hospital. I'm surprised because most doctors don't make it a habit of having their sleep interrupted like that unless it's an emergency."

Susan smiled. "Marc Carter is a different kind of doctor, Nancy. He seems to really care about his patients. They aren't just a number to him. And he sees mostly children, but he is the best neurosurgeon in the country. He could go anywhere and treat all kinds of patients, but he loves children."

"He seems like a real nice man, as well as a competent doctor." Nancy admitted as she finished packing up the few belongings that were in the room. Marc had said he would be there to make sure everything was okay with Sarah before she left, so she was expecting him to come anytime.

As if the thought itself brought him to life, Marc knocked on the partially closed door and said, "Can I come in?"

"It's Dr. Angel, Mommy. It's Dr. Angel!" Rushing to the door, Sarah opened it wide, greeting Marc with a huge grin, "Sure, come on in. Mommy and I have waited and waited a long time for you to come."

Marc laughed and knelt to look Sarah in the eyes. "And did you get some sleep like I said?"

"Oh yes, I went right to sleep. And I dreamed that I was such a good girl that Mommy bought me a puppy! Do you think dreams come true, Dr. Angel? 'Cause I sure hope so. I really want a puppy!"

"Whoa, Sarah, where did that come from?" Nancy asked in surprise. It was the first she had heard of the dream, but not the first time she had heard about a puppy.

Turning to her mother, Sarah placed her hands on her hips and said, "Well, Mommy, you said when we moved that maybe we could get a puppy. So we're moving to Auntie Susan's house, and that means that maybe we can have puppy."

Susan spoke up, "I'm sorry, princess, but I only rent. And I can't have any animals where I live. Maybe when you and your mommy find you a house, then you can have a puppy."

Sarah's shoulders drooped. "That will be a long, long time. Probably a 'undred years 'cause Mommy has to get a job, and then we have to save a bunch of money. It'll probably take a 'undred dollars to buy a house." She shook her head sadly as she went to pick up her backpack.

"Darling, I don't think it will take a hundred years, but when we do get a house of our very own, you can have a puppy." Nancy promised because she couldn't stand to see the hurt on Sarah's face. She had asked for a puppy almost since she had been able to talk. Joe would never even talk about getting a dog because he didn't like them.

With a happy look on her face, Sarah responded, "You cross you heart promise, Mommy?"

Nancy put an imaginary X over her heart and said, "I cross my heart, promise, Sarah."

"Goody! Now I know I'll get a puppy before a 'undred years." Turning to Marc, she said, "I'm ready to go now, Dr. Angel. Did you get all the papers ready so they say I can go home?"

"Well, I almost got them ready. I just need to do one more thing," Marc said.

"What's that?" Sarah asked.

"I need you to hop back on that bed and sit real still for me. I want to make sure you still have blue eyes," Marc teased.

Sarah crawled back on the bed and said, "You're silly. My eyes won't change colors. They've always been blue."

Marc got out his light so that he could shine it into each of Sarah's eyes and said, "Well, now I'm not so sure about that. I think I see some brown back there behind that blue…"

As he talked, he continued to look into her eyes and let his fingers gently touch Sarah's head, checking for any bumps that might have been missed.

"Sarah, look at my finger that I'm holding up," Marc said.

"Okay."

"Follow it with your eyes without turning your head. Can you do that?"

"Sure, that's easy," Sarah responded, but Marc noticed that one eye didn't follow exactly the way it should. It was only slight. If he hadn't been trained in neurology, he might never have picked up on it. Still, he knew that tests had showed nothing. He would recommend a few more tests to be done in his office.

"Well, princess, it looks like you are ready to get out of here and go to your aunt Susan's house," Marc said as he finished writing on the report. He also wrote down his office number so that Nancy could make an appointment with him to see Sarah in a couple of weeks.

"I'm ready, Dr. Angel," Sarah said, bouncing off the bed and getting her backpack again.

"Nancy, I'd like for you to make an appointment to see me in a couple of weeks. I'd like to see how Sarah is doing, and I'd like to schedule an MRI to be done."

Nancy took his card, sticking it into her purse. "I'll see what I can do, Doctor."

A nurse came in with a wheelchair and said, "Who's the lucky person that gets to ride in my race car?"

Sarah's eyes got big, and she said, "Is it me?"

The nurse smiled and replied, "I think it is. Hmmm, let me see." She checked the papers she held in her hand and said, "Are you Sarah Blackwell?"

"Yes, that's my name," Sarah said excited.

"Well, are you five years old?" the nurse continued.

"Yes! I'm five. Only real soon, I'll be this many!" Sarah said as she held up both of her hands with six fingers sticking straight out. "And I'll get to go to first grade."

"Well, that's wonderful! But this paper here says you have blond hair and blue eyes. Do you have blond hair and blue eyes?"

By this time, Sarah was jumping up and down, "Yes, yes, it's me, it's me!" Then she stopped. "But Dr. Angel said he saw some brown behind my blue eyes…it that okay?"

All of the adults laughed, and the nurse said, "Well, the doctor had a special light, so only he could see the brown. All I see is two pretty blue eyes, so hop on into the seat, and I'll race you downstairs. Let's see if we can beat your mom and your aunt, okay?"

"Yes!" Sarah said as she jumped into the wheelchair. "Yippee! I get to ride in a hospital race car! I didn't know that hospitals had race cars."

"Oh, we have lots of things that you don't know about. Maybe someday you'll get to see a lot of our secrets but not today." The nurse was saying as she wheeled Sarah out the door. Susan followed them toward the elevator. Nancy started to go also, but Marc stopped her with a gently hand on her arm.

"Nancy, I know you hesitated when I asked you to bring Sarah into my office. I know you're having trouble right now, and you don't have a job. But I'd really like to make sure that Sarah's okay in a couple of weeks. We'll work out something as for as the payment is concerned, but please bring her in."

Nancy's cheeks burned with embarrassment. It was so hard not having a job or the money to do the necessary things in life.

"I…I'll think about it. Maybe it would be better to wait until after I get a job. I'm planning on looking for a position that offers insurance as a benefit."

Marc pushed the issue. "That's all well and good, but I don't think you should wait. Sometimes it takes six months for a company to get their newest employees on healthcare insurance. And even then, the insurance companies are sticklers about what they cover. If this is a preexisting injury, they might turn it down."

"But—" Nancy interrupted.

Marc held up his hand and said, "Wait, we'll work out a payment plan that you'll be able to manage after you get a job. I don't want to wait longer than two weeks to do the MRI on Sarah."

"Did you find something that I should be worried about?"

"I didn't see anything on the CAT scan, but when I check her eyes, they don't react like I'd like for them too. It's very slight, and it could be absolutely nothing, but I would like to rule out every possibility of danger."

Nancy paled. "Danger? Could this be something serious?"

"Maybe I used too strong of a word…I just want to rule out anything that could possibly be wrong. Sarah's a beautiful little girl, and she has a long life ahead of her. I just want to make sure there's no trouble down the road for her. After all, she hit the pavement with her head, and it's better to be safe than sorry."

"All right, I'll give your office a call and set up an appointment, I promise."

"Cross your heart promise?" Marc said with a smile, remembering Sarah's words.

"Cross my heart promise," Nancy said as she again placed and X over her heart. Nancy smiled slightly, thinking about the man that stood in front of her. Why couldn't she have met someone like him, instead of someone like Joe? How different her life would have been. She turned and started toward the elevator, shaking the thought from her head. There was no sense wishing for something that didn't happen and never would.

Chapter 6

As Nancy arrived at the car, the nurse had just folded up the wheelchair and was saying goodbye to Sarah. "Now you take care of yourself, young lady, and make sure you mind your mother."

Sarah grinned up at the nurse from the backseat. "I always mind my mommy…well, most of the time."

The nurse laughed and looked at Nancy. "You've got a cutie there, Mrs. Blackwell."

"I know, and I think she knows it too!" Nancy smiled.

Laughing, the nurse pushed the wheelchair back inside while Nancy climbed into the passenger seat beside Susan.

As soon as Nancy got in the car, Sarah started chattering away, "Mommy, that 'ospital race car was the bestest! It went fast! Everybody got out of our way 'cause I went *beep, beep* like a horn. It was fun, Mommy. Can I do it again?"

Nancy glanced back at her daughter tucked safely into a car seat. "I don't know, Sarah. I hope you don't have to ride in it for anything but a good time. Mommy didn't like it when you were in the hospital."

"I know," the little girl responded wisely.

As Susan pulled away from the hospital, she asked, "What did Dr. Carter say?"

"He wants me to make an appointment for Sarah to see him in a couple of weeks."

"You're going to do that, aren't you?"

"Well…" Nancy hesitated.

"Nancy, I know you are worried about finances, but I know that Dr. Carter will work with you in paying the bill. He's done that before with other patients."

Nancy looked at her and asked, "How do you know that?"

Susan grinned. "I work at the hospital. Believe me when I say it's better than a newspaper!"

"But I don't want to be dependent upon anyone. I need to make my own way, Susan."

Susan glanced over at Nancy and then back at the road. She waited a few minutes and then said, "Do you remember the time that I had to come and live with you? It was about a year before you and Joe got married."

"Yes, I remember. You were in college and didn't have the money to pay your rent, so you got kicked out of your apartment."

"That's right. And you let me crash at your place until I could get a part-time job and get back on my feet. Right after that, you met Joe and got married."

Nancy remembered, but she didn't like talking about her marriage to Joe. It was something that didn't hold pleasant memories for her, but she had never told anyone, not even her sister, so she kept silent about it now.

"Nancy, you're going to have to learn to let people help you. I want to help. Dr. Carter wants to help. Don't fight everyone that wants to help. Everyone needs help sometimes in their lives."

"I know that. It's just that I was on my own for a while, and then I got married. Joe didn't want me to keep on working, so I quit, and then Sarah was born. I depended on Joe after I was married… and…and I just don't want to have to depend on anyone again." Nancy had depended on Joe, but Joe had let her down over and over. Now she was learning that it was best only to depend on yourself.

Susan turned down a street that was lined with houses on both sides and soon pulled into the driveway of a small brick home. "Well, here we are…home sweet home."

Nancy turned to say something to her daughter but noticed that Sarah was asleep with her head resting on the side of the car seat.

"Looks like Sarah is too tired to be excited about getting to Auntie Susan's house."

"Get her out, and I'll show you to your room so you can lay her on the bed. I hope you don't mind that you'll have to sleep with her, but I've only got two bedrooms."

"Sarah and I have been sleeping together for a while now. I would miss her if she wasn't with me," Nancy said as she got out of the car and unbuckled Sarah from her car seat.

Walking into the house was a relief from the heat of the day. The curtains were opened, but the air-conditioning was on, and it felt wonderful. Susan showed Nancy to her room and then went back outside to bring in the rest of the stuff.

Nancy eased Sarah down on the bed and smoothed back her hair. She looked at her beautiful daughter lying on the quilt that covered the bed. This was the only good thing to come out of my marriage, she thought.

Shaking her head, she tried to put the thoughts out of her mind. She didn't like thinking of Joe, of the things he did, or of the things he had said. She went out of the bedroom but left the door open in case Sarah woke up and was scared. Sometimes that happened when she was in a strange place.

Hearing Susan in the kitchen, she made her way there and watched as her sister got out some pots and pans to start cooking.

"When did you learn to cook?" Nancy teased.

"Oh, about the time I got real hungry and realized there was no fast-food places open, only grocery stores!" Susan teased back. "Actually, I took some cooking classes about a year ago, and I found that I enjoy cooking."

"That sounds like fun. I always wanted to take cooking classes, but Joe…" Nancy trailed off and didn't finish.

Susan looked at her sister and then said quietly, "Nancy, I know your marriage to Joe wasn't the best, so you don't have to pretend with me."

Nancy's head jerked up. "I've never said that Joe and I didn't have a good marriage."

"No, you didn't have to. It's the things that you didn't say that told me the story." Susan put a chicken in the oven to bake.

Taking down two glasses, she motioned for Nancy to sit down. "Go on and sit down, I'll get us some iced tea."

Sitting the glasses down on the table, Susan continued, "Before Dad died, Mom told me that you had come over there one night. She was worried because you had a large bruise on your cheek. You told her you had fallen down the front steps, but she didn't believe you, Nancy."

Nancy's face flamed with embarrassment. She remembered that night vividly. It was the only night she had gone to her parent's home. That day, she had found out she was pregnant with Sarah. She was so excited, and she couldn't wait until Joe came home from work so that she could tell him. They had never talked about having children, but Nancy had always wanted them. She had always dreamed of having two boys and two girls, and now it looked like her dream was starting to come true.

She had made a special dinner for Joe. She had even put candles on the table and had made his favorite roast. Joe was an hour late, but she knew sometimes he had to work late. So she kept the roast warm and waited for him patiently. Soon she heard his key in the door, and she turned to greet him. When she did, she could tell he had been drinking.

Nancy knew that Joe drank; she had known it before she married him, but she figured it wasn't very bad. And besides, he had come to church with her off and on while they were dating. She was sure that after they got married, he'd change. And he had changed, but it wasn't the change that she had wanted.

She could still see him as he came through the door and saw her standing there in one of his favorite dresses. She had fixed her hair and even put on some perfume.

"So what's the o…occasion?" Joe slurred his words.

"I dressed up for you, honey," Nancy said as she nervously wiped her hands down the front of her dress.

"For me? Now why would you dress up for me?" Joe staggered toward her. "I ain't nobody ssspecial. I'm just your husband."

"That's why I dressed up, you're my husband, and I wanted to dress up for you."

"You're lying!" he had screamed and grabbed her by her wrist, jerking her toward him. "You're dress'n up for somebody else, ain't ya? You met some other man…you think I don't know?"

"No, Joe! I haven't met anyone else," Nancy said. "Please, you're hurting me."

Joe struggled with her pushing her toward the door. "You don't want to live with me, then you can get outta here!"

"No, no, Joe, you don't know what you're saying. I'm not seeing anyone else…I'm…"

She didn't get to say anything else because he had opened the door and threw her down the steps. She had fallen hard and hit her face on the corner of the steps. She had blacked out for just a moment because when she opened her eyes, the door was shut, and she was alone in the dark, lying on the cold concrete.

Nancy could still feel the coldness that had seeped into not only her body that night but also her soul. She had prayed for Joe; she had been faithful to him. She had wanted God to change him, but God hadn't listened to her.

Pulling herself back to the present, she glanced at Susan who was waiting for her to say something.

"Well, I did fall down the steps. Joe…it was an accident… I…I don't want to talk about it."

"You don't have to tell me about it, Nancy, but I want you to know that I love you and care about you. Mom loves you too, and she is worried about you and Sarah. We both want you to go back to church. God cares about you, Nancy."

Sitting her glass down with a thump, Nancy responded, "Don't talk to me about how much God cares about me! If he had really cared about me, why didn't he stop Joe from…"

"Nancy, Joe can't hurt you anymore," Susan said quietly. "But if you allow him too, Joe can continue to rule your life even from the grave."

"No! I'm not going to let anyone rule my life anymore," Nancy declared as she got up from the table and walked over to look out at the darkening sky.

"God still cares about you, Nancy, and I won't stop telling you that because it's the truth."

"No…no, you're wrong, Susan. God doesn't care about me anymore…"

Her voice trailed off when she heard Sarah speak to her from the doorway, "Yes, he does, Mommy. The angel told me…and I believe him."

Nancy turned to see Sarah standing in the doorway, clutching her small pink Bible. She didn't know where she had found it. Because when she had laid her down, it wasn't beside her. She must have dug through her backpack and found the book.

"Sarah, did you have a good sleep?" Nancy said, trying to change the subject.

"Yes, but I had to find my Bible. It was hard," Sarah said as she walked over to the table. "Can I have some water? I'm really thirsty."

"Sure, honey, let me get you a glass of water. Or would you like some of my iced tea?" Susan said, getting up from the table.

"I like iced tea! Does it have sugar in it?" Sarah asked.

"Sure does. Why everyone knows that you can't make good iced tea without sugar!" Susan said, smiling as she poured Sarah a small glass.

Walking over and sitting the iced tea down in front of her, Susan said, "There you go, one glass of sweet iced tea just for my pretty niece."

Sarah picked up the glass and quickly finished it, "Can I have more?"

"Sarah, don't you think that's enough until supper?" Nancy said, not wanting her daughter to have a lot of sugar.

"But, Mommy, I'm really, really thirsty. Can I have water then?"

"Okay, let's get you some water instead," Susan said.

"Mommy, are we going to see Dr. Angel again soon?" Sarah asked innocently.

"I-I don't know, Sarah," Nancy stammered.

"Sure, you will, Sarah," Susan said. "Your mommy is going to make an appointment with him so that you will see him again in a couple of weeks."

"Goody! I like Dr. Angel. He's nice."

Nancy glared at Susan. Now she would have to make that appointment with Marc Carter or explain to her daughter why she didn't. She walked back to the bedroom, wondering if living with her sister was going to be the answer to her problems or just add to them. But right now, she didn't have any other options.

Chapter 7

For the next few days, Nancy helped Susan around the house as she and Sarah got settled in. Nancy did the housekeeping while Susan was at work. Sometimes she and Sarah would take a walk down the street where they lived. It wasn't long until Sarah had made friends with just about everyone on the street.

The beautiful little girl was very lively and never met a stranger. She was curious about everything that went on. The first person they met was an older woman, Mrs. Matthews, who lived down the street from them.

One morning, as Mrs. Matthews was sitting on her front porch, Nancy and Sarah walked by. Sarah skipped along singing a song she had just made up. Nancy hadn't seen the elderly lady in the shadows of her porch, but Sarah did.

"Hi, my name's Sarah, and this is my mommy, Nancy. We live with Auntie Susan in the yellow house down there. What's your name?" Sarah said it all without seeming to even take a breath.

Mrs. Matthews smiled a little and said, "My name is Nettie Matthews. It's nice to meet you, Sarah and Nancy." She slowly got up off her porch swing and started toward the steps.

When she came from the shadows, Sarah said, "Oh, you have a puppy!" She opened the gate before Nancy could stop her.

"Sarah, you shouldn't go into anyone's yard before they invite you," Nancy cautioned.

"But, Mommy, she has a puppy! I just want to see the puppy," Sarah said, never taking her eyes off the small dog that Mrs. Matthews was holding.

"Oh, my dear, I'm afraid that my Skippy isn't a puppy. He's old like me, and he can't see much anymore. So I carry him around because he keeps me company, and I keep him company." Mrs. Matthews took careful steps down to the sidewalk.

Nancy followed Sarah inside the gate and carefully closed it behind her. She watched as Sarah walked up to the elderly lady and said, "Can I pet the puppy?"

"Yes, but hold out your hand first and let him sniff you. If you'll do that and he learns your smell, he'll never forget you, and you can always pet him."

Sarah looked puzzled for a moment, but she did as Mrs. Matthews said. Her little hand lifted to the old dog's nose. Nancy watched as the gray muzzled dog sniffed it slowly. Then the dog's small tail began to wag.

"There, now Skippy knows just what you smell like, and he wants you to pet him," Nettie Matthews replied.

"He does?" Sarah asked incredulously. "How do you know?"

"Well, see his tail? It's wagging something fierce, and that means he's happy that he's met a new friend. He always likes for new friends to pet him."

"Oh," Sarah said as her hand gently pet the old dog on the head, and then she worked her way down to his neck and around under his chin. The dog continued to wag his tail as he raised his chin for her to scratch him.

"Be gentle, Sarah," Nancy admonished.

Impatiently, Sarah said, "I will, Mommy. I'm always careful with puppies."

Mrs. Matthews smiled down at Sarah and then at Nancy. "So you are living with Susan Montgomery? Susan had mentioned to me that her sister was coming to live with her. You must be her sister."

Nancy nodded. "Yes, I am. We just got here a few days ago. I plan on living here permanently, so I'm going to be looking for a job."

"How nice! I'm sure that Susan loves having you around. She's often told me about you and her darling niece. She told me that both of you were beautiful, but I must admit, I never figured you would both be as pretty as a picture!"

Nancy blushed. "Thank you, but Susan has been known to exaggerate. And in my case, I'm sure she did, but I'll take all the compliments about Sarah. I do think she is beautiful and the light of my life."

"I can tell that she is. But, dear, she looks just like you! So if you are going to admit that Sarah is beautiful, she'll look just like you someday, so that should tell you something."

Nancy started to respond when a voice behind her spoke. "Well, Aunt Nettie, you never told me that you knew Nancy and Sarah."

Turning quickly, Nancy looked into Marc Carter's eyes. Startled, she took a step backward and caught her shoe on the edge of the sidewalk. She stumbled slightly, and before she could right herself, Marc had grabbed her and steadied her. Marc was shocked at the feelings that went through him as the softness of her skin grazed his hand. As soon as she gained her footing, he let go, but her touch seemed to burn into his memory.

"Marc! I didn't expect you till later this evening. Do you know my new neighbors?" Nettie said as she watched with a gleam in her eye at Marc's reaction to Nancy. She had been praying for Marc for a while now. He just couldn't seem to let go of Melanie, or at least he didn't seem to want to date anyone or be interested in anyone... until now.

"Why don't all three of you come on in and get out of this sun? Goodness, I'm about to melt. I've got some iced tea just waiting for someone to drink! Oh, and now that I think about it...I've got some of my special sugar cookies that I'm sure Sarah would like with a glass of milk."

Sarah still didn't want to quit petting the "puppy," but she did stop for a minute to grin and say, "Hi, Dr. Angel."

"Hey there, princess," Marc replied. "How are you doing today."

"Good! Mommy and I were taking a walk when I saw Puppy and wanted to pet him. Did you know that Puppy sniffted my hand, and now he knows what I smell like?"

"Yep, Skippy likes to sniff people first and then make friends with them. He's a pretty good judge of character, so you must be a special young lady," Marc said as they all three made their way into the cool interior of the house.

Changing the subject, Sarah said, "I'm thirsty, Mommy. Can I have two glasses of milk?"

"No, honey, only one, but I'm sure you can have a glass of water," Nancy said, then turned to Marc.

"This hot sun must be really pulling the water from her body. She is always thirsty lately. We've only been gone for a half hour from the house, and she drank two glasses of water there."

Marc glanced at Sarah and then said, "Could be the heat. Does she go to the bathroom a lot too?"

Nancy laughed a little and said, "Oh yes, she can't pass a bathroom without stopping. I'm surprised she hasn't needed to go yet. I'm sure it won't be long before she'll be asking. We were only going to walk around the block because it's too hot to go to the park, but we met your aunt, and Sarah loves dogs."

Marc smiled and nodded, then almost like it was an afterthought, he said, "Have you made that appointment yet?"

Nancy blushed and stammered, "N-no, not...not yet. I will though."

"Okay, I'll hold you to it. After all, you crossed your heart promised," he said as he made an X over his heart.

Smiling, Nancy said, "You can't break a cross your heart promise."

Just then Sarah glanced over at Nancy and saw the smile on her face. Beaming up at Marc, Sarah said, "See, Dr. Angel, it's just like I said. Mommy is smiling again. You got her to smile."

Nancy choked back a burst of laughter, and Marc cleared his throat as Mrs. Matthews said, "Well now, this conversation sounds real interesting. So let's sit down and have some refreshments, and you can tell me the whole story."

Marc decided the best thing to do was just to tell Aunt Nettie exactly how he and Nancy Blackwell had met. It was easier that way because then his aunt wouldn't speculate on all the *maybes* in his life, such as, maybe Marc would start dating again, or maybe Marc would get interested in Nancy. Aunt Nettie was good at trying to get him to see things her way.

He told his aunt about the accident at the bus station and the hospital visit with Nancy adding a few things here and there. Aunt Nettie said, "Goodness, thank God, you were in the right place at the right time. God sure seems to have a way of working things out for our good, doesn't he?"

Marc grimaced as he heard his aunt, knowing that she was already thinking about him and Nancy. He glanced over at Nancy to see if she caught on to what his aunt was saying, and she must have because of the frown on her face. He wondered why Nancy would think it would be such a distasteful idea.

Nancy heard Mrs. Matthews mentioned the fact that God was in the accident. Why did everyone have to always put God in everything that was done? She glanced over at Marc to see how he was responding and saw him glancing at her.

Turning to Sarah who was quietly drinking her second glass of water, she said, "Honey, you seem to be doing good now. Do you still feel okay?"

Sarah grinned and set the glass down on the table as she said, "Yes, Mommy and I are doing great 'cause Jesus healed me. And the angel said that Mommy was going to laugh again, and that means she's going to be happy."

Marc knew that Aunt Nettie would never let a chance to talk about the Lord go by, so she said, "Jesus healed you, and an angel talked to you? Goodness, child, I want you to tell me all about it."

Sarah was delighted to have a completely captive audience; she started in retelling the story of the car hitting her and how an angel had picked her up and held her hand and what he had told her.

"Do you believe in angels, Auntie Nettie?" Sarah asked innocently.

"That's Mrs. Matthews, Sarah," Nancy corrected.

"No, no, let the child call me Auntie Nettie! It has a certain ring to it, don't you think?"

"Goody, now I have two aunties! Auntie Susan and now Auntie Nettie."

"It's always nice to have lots and lots of aunties," Marc commented. He knew that almost everyone called his aunt, Aunt Nettie. She was known around town as everyone's aunt or grandmother.

"Sarah," Aunt Nettie said, "since you've talked to an angel, how would you like to go to Sunday school with me this Sunday?"

"Sunday school? I like Sunday school. Auntie Susan told me that she would take me to her Sunday school too." Suddenly Sarah's face got sad. "But if I go to Auntie Susan's Sunday school, then I can't go to yours."

"Oh, child, don't you worry about that because your Auntie Susan goes to my Sunday school too!"

"She does?" Sarah asked in awe.

"Yes, she does. Why she's been going to my Sunday school for a long time now, so since you are going with her, I'll get to see you too." Nettie Matthews was glad that Susan was already making sure that Sarah was coming to church.

Glancing over at Nancy, she said, "You're coming too, aren't you?"

"I…I, well, I thought I would let Susan take Sarah this Sunday. I need to catch up on a lot of things, and I…" Nancy stammered.

"Nonsense, child! Sundays are a day of rest and a day to worship the Lord. Everyone needs at least one day a week for that. There's nothing that you have to do that can't wait until Monday."

Nancy didn't really have a good excuse for not going this Sunday, so she said, "I guess I can make it then." She figured if she went once, then her obligation was complete, and she wouldn't have to worry about every Sunday.

"Goody! Jesus did hear my prayers. I prayed that Mommy would go with me to Sunday school, and she's going!" Sarah said as she finished off her glass of water.

Nancy glanced over at her daughter in amazement. She never knew that Sarah even knew how to pray, much less prayed for her! Her mind went back to the few times that she had knelt beside Sarah's bed and prayed that God would protect them. That was when she still believed that prayer worked…back before Joe got so bad.

Sarah suddenly sprang from her chair and whispered into her mom's ear. Nancy smiled slightly and said, "Could we borrow your bathroom for a few minutes?"

"But, Mommy, I don't need to borrow it…I need to use it," Sarah said as she danced around.

All the adults laughed as Nettie showed them where to find the bathroom. While Sarah and Nancy were occupied, Nettie returned to the table and said, "Such a sweet little girl! And her mother is a beauty!"

Marc sighed; he knew exactly what his aunt was pushing at him, "Yes, Sarah is a very sweet little girl."

"And what about Nancy?" Aunt Nettie pushed.

"She seems to really care about her daughter a lot, and that is commendable for a—" Marc didn't get to finish what he was about to say before his aunt interrupted.

"Phish! You know exactly what I am talking about, Marc Carter, and don't you try to fishtail around it!"

"Yes, Aunt Nettie, I know exactly what you are saying and exactly what you are trying to do. It hasn't worked in the past, and it won't work this time either."

"Now, Marc, you are completely discounting what God can do in your life! Why, it just might be his will that Nancy has come along when she did. It's time for you to start living again. Melanie would never have liked for you to go this long without finding someone to love."

"I did find someone to love, and it was Melanie. It will always be Melanie, Aunt Nettie," Marc spoke gently because even though he was frustrated at his aunt, he also loved her and knew she wanted what was best for him.

"Marc, it was Melanie, and I'm so glad that you had a wonderful wife who loved you as much as she did, but Melanie isn't here any longer. And you are much too young to live the rest of your life alone. I know from experience that time changes things."

"Time doesn't diminish love, Aunt Nettie. I will always love Melanie and Amber. No one can take their place in my heart."

"And any woman that tried would be a complete fool for doing so! I'm not talking about anyone taking Melanie and Amber's place." She reached over and laid her hand over Marc's on the table. "Marc, no one can take their place in your heart, but that is the wonderful thing about us that God made. He made our hearts to expand. We can make a place in our hearts for each and every one that comes our way. Some come our way for only a little while, but they leave their imprint upon our hearts. It will always be there just like your footprint in the wet cement out there on the sidewalk."

Marc glanced over at his aunt and listened.

"Do you remember making that footprint?" When he nodded, she continued, "You were only four years old. You had such a tiny footprint then, and I remember how you laughed as the wet cement squished up between your toes. Your uncle James delighted in that footprint! He made sure it was kept there no matter what. But, Marc, do you see how much different your footprint would be today if you were to make one in wet cement again? It would be bigger, and although it may still have some of the same characteristics of your small footprint, it has changed. Your heart is the same way. Melanie and Amber left footprints on your heart, but as the time passes, things change. The next set of footprints will be different, but no less real…if you will allow love to come in again."

"Aunt Nettie, we've went over this before. I'm just not ready..." His voice trailed off as he heard Sarah and Nancy coming back down the hallway.

Nancy came into the room, and the sunlight from the kitchen window fell upon her. The light seemed to surround her for just a moment, and to Marc, she was beautiful! He knew she had always been lovely, but this time he was struck by her beauty. Mentally shaking himself again, he tried to remember Melanie and how she looked with the sun shining on her, but for some reason, he couldn't. He could see her face plainly but couldn't remember the sun in her hair. It frustrated him that his memories were fading away.

Nancy didn't realize what had been said or what was going on in Marc's mind. Stepping forward, she gathered up her glass and Sarah's putting them in the sink and said, "Thank you so much, Mrs. Matthews, for the tea and the cookies. The tea was so refreshing, and the cookies were wonderful! Sarah and I need to be getting back home. I didn't realize it was so late. Susan will be home and wondering where we are."

Marc stood up and said, "I've got to be going too, Aunt Nettie. I've got some calls to make, and I still need to make my rounds at the hospital this evening."

Glancing over at Nancy and Sarah, he said, "Let me give you a ride home."

Nancy grinned. "Oh, that's not necessary since we only live a few houses down from here."

Sarah pulled on her mom's blouse and said, "But, Mommy, Dr. Angel probably had a chariot! Angels have chariots you know, and I've always wanted to ride in one. Please can we ride in Dr. Angel's chariot?"

"Sarah, Dr. Carter does not have a chariot. He has a car, just like everyone else. And it won't hurt us to walk back. It's just a little ways."

"But, Mommy," Sarah whined a little. "I'm hot and tired. I don't want to walk back to Auntie Susan's, I want to ride."

"Oh, all right," Nancy said as she gave in. She wouldn't have done it normally, but Susan had been tired a lot lately, and she didn't want her to have a relapse from the accident. Looking up at Marc, she said, "I guess you can be our chauffeur for today."

They walked toward the front door with Mrs. Matthews trailing behind with Skippy in her arms. Sarah suddenly stopped and said, "Just a minute, Mommy."

Walking back to Mrs. Matthews, she touched the old dog gently and then stood on tiptoe and pressed her face into his fur. Taking a deep breath, then she turned away and smiled.

"What was that all about, young lady?" Nancy questioned.

"The puppy wanted to know what I smelled like so that he would remember me, so I wanted to know what he smelled like so I would remember him!" Sarah said matter-of-factly.

"And what did he smell like?" Marc asked.

Sarah frowned a little and then brightened, "Sorta like perfume!"

"Well, I'll tell you a secret," Mrs. Matthews said in a loud whisper. "I just gave Skippy his bath, and I sprayed some of my perfume on him, but don't ever tell him because it is girl's perfume, and he's a boy. He might not like it."

Sarah made an X over her heart and said, "I cross my heart promise I won't tell him!"

With a laugh and a smile, they all made their way outside. Marc helped Nancy and Sarah into the car, helping Sarah buckle her seatbelt in the back seat. Waving goodbye to his aunt standing on the porch, he jumped into the car and backed out of the driveway.

Watching them go, Nettie Matthews smiled. "Well, Lord, you did it again. I've prayed and prayed for that young man to find a good woman again. And here I couldn't think of one woman here that would make him a good wife. I just didn't put enough faith in you that you could bring it about."

Looking down at Skippy, she scratched the old dog behind the ears. He looked up toward her as she spoke, "Well, Skippy, I think we need to do some more praying because I think the Lord is going to have to hit Marc over the head with a two-by-four before he will acknowledge his interest in Nancy. But you know what, old friend? The Lord knows just how to do it!"

Chapter 9

The alarm went off on Sunday morning, and Marc groaned as he reached over and slapped the snooze button. He snuggled down under the sheet again for only a couple of seconds and then realized that he needed to make rounds before he went to church.

Getting out of bed, he put on his suit pants, shirt, and tie and headed out the door. As he reached his car, he thought about Nancy. She had promised Aunt Nettie that she would be in church today; he was looking forward to seeing her and Sarah. He told himself it was really Sarah he wanted to see, but it was Nancy's face that kept coming into his mind.

Pulling his car into a "reserved for physicians" parking spot, he got out and shut the door, hurrying into the double doors. He wanted to make sure he was at the church when Nancy came in. He didn't think she knew he went to the same church or that he even went to church. So he wanted to be sure she saw him there.

After seeing the three patients that he had in the hospital, he went into the nurse's station to make a change in a patient's medications. As he walked in, Mary was coming out of the break room with her coat and purse in her hands. "Hi, Dr. Carter!"

"Hello, Mary, I thought you worked days."

"I usually do, but Rebecca called in sick, so the nurse manager asked me if I would pull a nightshift last night. So I'm just getting off work. How come you're here so early today?"

"I'm here because I'm going to church after I get through with these charts. I've got to go and pick up my aunt who lives on the corner of Thirty-First and Jefferson Street. It's a little ways from here, but it's on my way to church, and I promised her a ride today." Marc didn't add that he hoped he could offer a ride to his aunt's neighbors also.

"Your aunt lives on the corner of Thirty-First and Jefferson? She must be the one that has that darling white house with all the roses!"

"Yep, that's Aunt Nettie. She's always loved her roses. I give her a new one every birthday, and she seems to have a green thumb when it comes to growing them."

"Your aunt only lives a couple of blocks from my apartment."

"Do you live in those new apartments they built over by the park?"

"Yep, those are the ones." Mary hesitated and then squared her shoulders and said, "Uh, Dr. Carter, I haven't been to church in quite a while. Would you mind swinging by and picking me up and letting me go with you and your aunt this morning?"

Marc stopped. He knew that Mary had been showing interest in him for a long time now, and he didn't want to encourage it. Although Mary was a lovely young woman, she didn't interest Marc in the same way that…well, that Melanie had interested him, his mind shying away from the name Nancy. But he couldn't very well tell Mary she couldn't come to church with him, so he said, "Sure, Mary, I'll pick up Aunt Nettie first and then swing by your place. What number do you live in?"

Mary's smile grew bigger as she said, "I'm in number 8 on the bottom floor! I'll hurry home now and be ready when you get there. Thanks, Dr. Carter."

Marc watched her hurry off as he sighed. Now he didn't know what to do. How would Aunt Nettie take it that he was taking a woman to church? He knew his aunt had wanted him to get interested in someone else for a long time now. What she didn't know was how Nancy's presence seemed to reach out to him, but he couldn't let anything happen between him and Nancy. He just wasn't ready for another relationship yet, he argued with himself.

Susan was up early on Sunday morning, humming "Amazing Grace" as she fixed breakfast for the three of them. She reached over and picked up a cup and filled it with coffee. She looked toward the kitchen door as Nancy came in yawning.

"Boy, you're up early, and you sound happy. What's the occasion?" Nancy said after she had quit yawning.

"Nothing really, it's just that I enjoy Sunday mornings. I don't have to go to work, and I get to go to church," Susan said with a smile as she handed a second cup of coffee to Nancy.

Nancy took it gratefully, sitting down at the table and sipping. The hot brew felt good going down her throat, and she knew that the caffeine would be great to wake her up.

"And besides, look outside," Susan said. "It's a beautiful morning, the sun is shining, and the birds are singing."

Nancy had been looking out the patio doors, and as she became more awake, she said, "Well, you're right about that. It is a beautiful morning, and the birds are singing. I can hear them all the way through the glass doors." Nancy leaned over and watched the twittering creatures as they sang and jump from limb to limb.

"Speaking of singing," Nancy continued, "what was the song you were humming when I came in? It sounded like 'Amazing Grace'."

"It was, although I'm no singer," Susan responded ruefully. "But I was just thinking about all that God has done for me and how he has blessed me, and I couldn't help but hum that tune."

"I don't get it. How can you sing about how much God has done for you when you look at your life?"

"What do you mean?" Susan questioned.

"Well, for one, you don't have a new car. Yours is on the brink of dying. You are renting this house, so you can't even call that your own...and...well, you don't even have a boyfriend. You've never been married and still don't have a boyfriend. How can you say that God has been good to you?"

"I don't base the goodness of God on things, Nancy. God is good to me to allow me to be able to get up this morning, to be able to hum a tune to him, and to be able to go to church today. Those are all blessings from God. If we based how we feel about God, on what we have, then we will never love God or praise him. A lot of people are very selfish, and they can only thank God when things are going their way, but that's not the way God wants us to do it. He wants us to love him…just because."

"I guess I just don't get it."

"Okay, how about this? Do you want Sarah to love you because you buy her princess stuff and pretty things? Do you want her to love you because you buy her the toys she wants? Or do you want her to love you because you are her mother, and you love her?"

"Of course, I want Sarah to love me because I am her mother, and I love her. But because I love her, I buy her those things."

"But what about now? Since you don't have a lot of money and you can't buy her those things, do you want her to stop loving you?"

"That's completely silly. Of course, I don't!"

"That is the same way with God. Not that he couldn't give me the things that I desire, but sometimes it is best if we don't get everything we want. God knows what is best for us, and it isn't good to want something for our lives that he doesn't want for our lives. It could and probably would lead to problems or trouble."

"Like a boyfriend?" Nancy pushed.

"Actually, I do sort of have a boyfriend. Or at least I think he likes me, and I really like him."

Nancy smiled. She was glad that Susan liked someone. She had always wanted her sister to find a man who would love and cherish her because she was a great person, and she had so much love to give. "Who's the lucky man?"

"Well, I'll let you see him at church, and I'll give you a hint…his name is Mark. But that is all I'm telling you until we get to church."

Suddenly Nancy's stomach started churning. Did Susan say Marc? Could it be possible that Susan and Marc Carter liked each other? Nancy considered it for a few minutes and realized that Susan worked at the hospital, and Marc was there a lot. It wouldn't be hard for those two to get together at all.

But they are so wrong for each other, Nancy reasoned, then felt ashamed. Who was she to know who was right for each other? She had thought that Joe was right for her and look how wrong she had been.

Getting up from the table, Nancy said, "Well, I had better get Sarah up and start getting us both ready for church. Turning, she walked out of the kitchen, leaving Susan staring after her.

I wonder what in the world is wrong with her. Surely, she isn't upset because I have a boyfriend, and she doesn't, Susan thought. Shaking her head, she picked up Nancy's coffee cup and went to the sink to rinse them both out. After she was finished, she headed to her bedroom to get ready to go to church too. Mark popped into her mind, and she smiled. He was a good man, and maybe someday they might be a family. She would just have to see what God worked out.

Marc drove to his aunt's house. Looking down the street, he could see Nancy, Sarah, and Susan getting into Susan's car. All three were dressed for church, but his eyes rested on Nancy. She looked good in the summer dress that she wore. It seemed to enhance her already perfect figure, and he found his eyes watching her gracefully get in her car and shut the door.

He pulled into his aunt's driveway and got out, walking up through the gate, just as Susan drove by, and gave a little honk with the car horn. He turned and waved, noticing that Susan waved, and Sarah smiled out the side window, waving frantically at him. Nancy smiled slightly, then turned her head back toward the front, effectively dismissing him.

Slightly miffed at her reaction but not knowing exactly why, he started to knock on the door when Aunt Nettie opened it.

"Hello there, Marc, I heard a car horn out here and thought you were blowing the horn at me to hurry."

"I've never done that before, Aunt Nettie. Why would I start now? We're not that late."

"I didn't look at the clock. I just heard the horn. Who was it that was blowing the horn anyway?"

"It was Susan Montgomery. She was just driving by on her way to church."

Aunt Nettie looked down the road as if she could still see them. "Was Nancy and Sarah with her?" she asked innocently.

Something in her voice caused Marc to look at her as he helped her get into the car. "I think you know they were both with her, Aunt Nettie."

He didn't hear her reply as he shut the door and walked around to the driver's side. Getting in, he started the car and said, "I've got to pick up someone for church myself. She said she would be ready when I got there."

"She?" Aunt Nettie asked with a raised eyebrow.

"Yes, ma'am. Her name is Mary Landers, and she's a nurse at the hospital." Marc waited until he had pulled out onto the road before he glanced over at his aunt. He noticed she had a slight frown on her face.

"What's wrong? Aren't you glad I'm picking up a young lady, and she's going to church with me?" Marc teased.

"Well, of course, I'm glad. You're doing your Christian duty by bringing someone to church. Goodness, we all need to do that." Aunt Nettie dodged the question artfully.

Marc smiled as he pulled into the parking space in front of apartment number 8. Getting out of his car, he walked up and knocked on Mary's door. It quickly opened, and Mary stood, waiting for him. She had changed out of her nurse's uniform and into a black dress that fit her like a glove. It was a little too low-cut for Marc's comfort, but who was he to say what a woman should wear to church?

"Ready to go?" Marc asked unnecessarily.

"Oh yes, I'm looking forward to going," Mary said as she hooked her arm into Marc's even though he had not offered it.

Walking her around to the backseat, he opened the door and noticed that Mary had frowned slightly when she realized she wasn't going to be sitting up front with him. Oh well, he thought, she was just going to have to accept the fact that Aunt Nettie gets the front seat.

Gracefully Mary got in, making sure that she kept her leg out a little longer than necessary, knowing that the slit in her dress showed off a long length of her leg to Marc. Slowly she slipped her leg inside and smiled as Marc shut the door. She was sure he had gotten a good look at her bare leg, and if Marc was like other men, she was sure he had enjoyed it.

Marc walked around to the driver's door and got in, slamming it a bit harder than necessary. He was disgusted already. He wished he would have let one of the ladies from the church come and pick Mary up instead of him. He had noticed Mary's long leg slipping from the slit in her dress, but instead of enticing him, it had actually frustrated him.

His mind went to Nancy and how he had made himself look away as her skirt rose slightly as it skimmed her knees getting into Susan's car. He had wanted to keep looking but felt it wasn't right, so he had turned his head. Why had he wanted to look at Nancy and yet was disgusted at what Mary had done? He refused to keep thinking about it, instead he started thinking about one of the patients at the hospital.

"Marc, are you listening to me?" Aunt Nettie spoke loudly to him.

"Ah…huh? What? I'm sorry, Aunt Nettie. I had my mind on a patient at the hospital," he answered truthfully.

"I said you never introduced me to your friend," Aunt Nettie reprimanded him.

"I'm sorry. It completely slipped my mind." Glancing at Mary in the rearview mirror, he said, "Aunt Nettie, this is Mary Landers. Mary, this is my aunt, Mrs. Matthews."

"Hello, dear," Aunt Nettie said, turning slightly in her seat. "It's so nice that you wanted to come to church with us today. I'm sure you will enjoy the service, and our pastor is wonderful."

"I'm excited to be going today. I usually work at the hospital on Sunday mornings, so I don't get to go to church very often. Since I worked the night shift and met Dr. Carter this morning, it seemed like the perfect opportunity when he mentioned he was going."

"Oh, don't call him Dr. Carter here, dear. Why he's just Marc Carter away from the hospital. After all, he's not your boss here!"

Marc sighed. "I'm not her boss at the hospital either, Aunt Nettie. I'm just one of the doctors there. Mary works for the hospital, not for me."

A few minutes later, Marc pulled into the circle drive at the church that allowed drivers to drop off their passengers. It was very convenient especially for the elderly and when it was raining. It was especially convenient today since Marc could drop both ladies off together. He knew that Aunt Nettie would find them a seat, and he wouldn't have to walk in with Mary.

Chapter 10

Nancy and Susan sat near the front of the large church. Nancy glanced around and noticed the stained glass windows and the plush carpets. It was a beautiful church, made to make everyone feel comfortable. She wondered why it was that she felt so uncomfortable there.

Susan tapped Nancy on the arm. "I want you to meet someone, Nancy."

Turning toward Susan, she saw a tall man with light-blond hair, smiling down at them. He had an engaging smile and nice eyes. He stuck his hand out and said, "I've wanted to meet you, Mrs. Blackwell. Susan has been looking forward to your coming for a long time. I'm Mark Siders, a friend of Susan's."

The way he looked at Susan made Nancy think that he wanted to be more than her friend. Then it hit her. *This is the Mark that Susan was talking about this morning!* It wasn't Marc Carter at all. Feelings of relief washed over her, then bewilderment hit. Why did she care? She wondered. If Susan would have liked Marc Carter, it wouldn't have mattered…would it?

"It's nice to meet you, Mark. I'm glad that Susan wasn't worried about me coming to live with her." Nancy smiled as she shook his hand.

"Not at all. In fact, she was so excited that I've not been able to see much of her since she was getting the room ready for you and your daughter," Mark said.

"Well, I'm here now, and the room is perfect. So maybe you can come around more often. I'm sure Susan would enjoy the company," Nancy said and smiled as she felt Susan kick her on the shoe.

Outside, Marc reached for the handle of the clear-glass church door and walked into the cool air-conditioned building. It felt so good, even this early in the morning. It was going to be another scorcher outside today, Marc figured as his eyes adjusted to the dimmer light of the church. Glancing around, he saw the greeters in the foyer and shook their hand as one of them handed him a bulletin that was given to everyone as they came in the door.

As he walked into the double doors of the sanctuary, he looked over toward where Susan usually sat, and sure enough, there was Susan and Nancy sitting together. Susan was talking to Mark Siders, and Nancy was smiling. He glanced around for Sarah before realizing that she was probably already in her Sunday school classroom. He would see her later, he reasoned.

Casually walking down the aisle that would take him past Susan and Nancy, he glanced over and saw that his aunt and Mary were sitting on the opposite side of the church. He was a little frustrated with that because usually his aunt liked sitting in the row right in front of where Nancy and Susan were sitting. Sighing, he thought to himself, she would pick today to sit elsewhere.

As he walked by, he heard Susan say, "Good morning, Dr. Carter, how are you today?"

Turning with a smile, he said, "I'm good, Susan. How are you and your family?" Holding his hand out to Mark, he said, "Hi, Mark, how's business going?"

"Pretty good, now that you're here." Mark rejoined with a laugh.

Susan spoke up, "I heard that you saw Nancy and Sarah at Mrs. Matthew's yesterday. I'm glad they got to meet your aunt."

"Yes, she enjoyed meeting them too," Marc said as he glanced over at Nancy. He noticed that she kept looking down at her hands but, every once in a while, would glance his direction. He wondered if she was worried that he would say something about remembering to make an appointment to see him. He decided not to say anything today. After all, this was church, so instead he said, "Nancy, how are you and Sarah doing?"

Looking up, she said, "We are both doing fine. Sarah keeps talking about your 'chariot' and her Auntie Nettie having a puppy named Skippy."

"Good. I'm glad she's thinking about us. She's a cutie, and I think she loves animals…especially dogs."

Nancy rolled her eyes and said, "You just don't know how much. She's been begging me for a dog ever since she knew we were going to be moving to Susan's. I've put her off until we get a place of our own, but when we do, there will be no way to take care of a dog and work too…I'm just hoping that she will forget it."

"Somehow, I doubt that she does that," Marc said. Then looking at his watch, he said, "Service is about to start. I'd better go sit with Aunt Nettie. I'll see you all later." He nodded at Susan and Nancy and gave Mark a grin. "Don't you think you need to get busy?"

"Looks like it," Mark replied as he turned to walk up on the platform.

Nancy leaned over to Susan and said, "Mark is nice. What kind of business does he do?"

"You'll see real soon." Susan promised.

Nancy was puzzled, but instead of watching Mark Siders, she couldn't keep her eyes off the tall, broad-shouldered man in the perfectly tailored white shirt that was making his way over to Nettie Matthews. She saw Marc sit down next to a dark-haired young woman in a black dress, and she also watched as a slight frown marred Marc's feature. But the woman leaned over and said something to him, which caused him to laugh, and Nancy saw a triumphant look cross the woman's face as she settled back into her seat.

I wonder who she is, Nancy thought. But then her attention was caught by a familiar voice that said, "Could we all stand and pray?" Looking up, she saw Mark Siders standing behind the pulpit.

Glancing over at Susan, she whispered, "Is Mark the pastor?"

Susan grinned and said, "Yes, he is…and he's a good one too."

Nancy's attention wondered again during the prayer as she couldn't keep her eyes off Marc and the woman in black. When the singing started, she noticed that the woman shared the songbook with Marc and seemed to lean into him every chance she got.

Nancy whispered to Susan as they sat down. "Who's the woman sitting beside Dr. Carter?"

Susan glanced over that way and said, "Oh, that's Mary Landers. She's been after Marc ever since she started working at the hospital. Looks like she finally got him to notice her."

Nancy felt something slam against her heart. So this was a woman who was interested in the handsome doctor. Mentally kicking herself, she thought, *So what? He doesn't mean anything to me. He is just Sarah's doctor and nothing more.* Firmly she got her mind on what the pastor was saying, determined not to think about Marc Carter or the beautiful and seductive woman who was sitting almost in his lap.

Chapter 11

After service, Marc found that Mary clung to him like glue. He wanted to make his way back to Nancy, but he didn't want to have Mary with him. Aunt Nettie was talking to Mrs. Waterman about her garden, and he couldn't get her attention.

Resigned to his fate, Marc decided it would be best if he were to introduce her to others. After all, it was his Christian duty to see that Mary enjoyed the church service enough to come back. He didn't know if she was a Christian or not, but if she wasn't, this was a chance to get her to know the people at the church.

Letting her hold on to his arm, they made their way through the crowded church and out into the foyer. Marc was greeted several times, and each time he introduced Mary to the person talking to him. Just as Mr. Winegart left, Marc glanced up and saw Nancy and Susan headed his way. Well, actually they were probably making their way to the outside, but he was standing by the door, so they would have to go past him.

Nancy held Sarah's hand as they slowly made their way to the entrance. Sarah was babbling away about the fun she had had in Sunday school. She showed Nancy her coloring paper that she had done. It was a picture of Baby Moses in the bulrushes, and she had colored it pretty good for a four-year-old.

"Mommy, guess what? Did you know that Baby Moses had to be put in a basket? He went to sleep and woke up when a bad lady found him, and then he was crying 'cause the woman was bad and not his mommy. I'd cry if some other woman found me if you put me in a basket. Would you ever lose me, Mommy? 'Cause if you did,

I'd start crying right away. That way someone would see me crying and ask me, 'Little girl, who is your mommy' Then I'd tell them it was Nancy Blackwell, and they would find you for me. Isn't that right, Mommy?"

Nancy was half listening but caught the last part and said, "That's good, Sarah, but if you always stay with me like I told you, then you won't ever be lost."

"But I don't want you to put me in a basket 'cause it would be terrible to be inside a basket with the lid all shut up and floating on the water."

"I'm sure it would, Sarah. Let's hurry now. Auntie Susan is wanting to get home because she is having company."

"Really? Is it Dr. Angel? Is he coming over to see us? I want to ride in his chariot again and—" Sarah stopped and then pointed toward the door. "Look, Mommy, there's Dr. Angel right over there. Let's go talk to him."

Before Nancy could stop her, Sarah let go of her hand and rushed toward where Marc was standing. Nancy had already seen him and the black-haired woman who stood beside him. She was hoping to make her way through the doors in the crowd and miss them altogether.

She sighed. It looked like that wasn't going to happen now. She watched as Marc bent down and was talking to Sarah. She saw her daughter nod and then point back at her. *I might as well go on and talk to him. Sarah isn't going to let me get off that easy*, she thought.

Squaring her shoulders, she made her way over to where her daughter stood. Marc turned and smiled, holding out his hand. "I'm glad you made it to church today, Nancy. I certainly hope you'll be back."

Nancy glanced down at Sarah and then said, "Well, if Sarah has anything to do with it, we will be back. Besides, I actually enjoyed the pastor's sermon this morning. And it seems that we are having him over for dinner today."

"That's good. He's fun to be around. I think you'll enjoy having him," Marc said.

"Yes, I enjoyed talking with him this morning before service." Nancy reached down and grabbed Sarah's hand and said, "Well, we've got to go. Susan wants to get home and finish up dinner before the pastor gets there."

"Wait," Marc said, remember Mary beside him. "I'd like for you to meet Mary Landers. She is a nurse at the hospital, and she wanted to come to church this morning. Mary, this is Nancy Blackwell and her daughter, Sarah."

Nancy put a smile on her face. "It's nice to meet you, Mary," she said as she shook her hand. "At least I wasn't the only visitor here today."

Mary smiled, but it didn't quite reach her eyes. "It's nice to meet you too. And I enjoyed the service also. I'm hoping that Marc will continue to come and pick me up for church as much as possible. It was so sweet of him to offer today."

Nancy nodded slightly, then spoke to Sarah, "Come on, honey. Auntie Susan is probably in the car, waiting on us." Turning to both Marc and Mary, she said her goodbyes and hurried away, towing a very reluctant Sarah behind her.

After settling Sarah in her car seat, she climbed in the passenger side. "Sorry we're late getting here. Marc Carter stopped us and chatted a few minutes."

Sarah spoke up, "And he had another lady with him. Is that his girlfriend, Auntie Susan?"

Nancy held her breath while Susan said, "I don't know, princess. It could be, but somehow I doubt it. I've seen Mary Landers around the hospital, and she doesn't ever seem to be around Dr. Carter that much." Looking over at Nancy, she added, "Not that she doesn't want to be, but Marc seems to steer clear of women who are trying to latch on to him."

"I don't think he's trying too hard to stay away from her. She even mentioned that Marc would probably keep picking her up for church."

"Hmmm, that's interesting. I wonder whose idea it was that she even come to church? Not that I don't think it is good because everyone needs to go to church, but I just wonder how it all happened," Susan said as she turned down their street.

"Well, from what she said, it was Marc's idea," Nancy said with a slight edge to her voice.

Susan glanced over at Nancy, catching the slight change in her tone. She didn't show any outward emotion, but she was smiling on the inside. Just to think that Nancy might be slightly jealous of Mary Landers! Nancy deserved someone like Marc Carter. After having to put up with what Joe put her through, Marc would treat her like the special person she really was.

Pulling into the driveway, the three of them hurried into the house to prepare the meal for the pastor who was coming over.

As Marc drove away from the church, Aunt Nettie was sitting firmly in the front seat again, even though she protested. He was determined that Mary was not going to sit up front. Besides, he reasoned, he was dropping off Mary first anyway, so it only made sense.

"Marc, dear, would you mind dropping me off first? Mrs. Waterman is coming over, and I want to make sure I'm home when she gets there. She wants to look at my roses. I'm going to give her a cutting from the Peace rose so that she can try to start her own," Aunt Nettie said.

Marc gritted his teeth. "Mary only lives about five minutes from you, Aunt Nettie. I'm sure we will have plenty of time to drop her off and get you home before Mrs. Waterman gets there."

"Well, if you think so, dear," Aunt Nettie said sweetly.

Marc got to Mary's apartment, and even though he didn't want to, he got out and opened the door for Mary to get out of the car. She smiled sweetly up at him and said, "Thank you so much for taking me to church, Marc. I do hope you don't mind if I catch a ride with you again sometimes?"

"No, no, that will be fine. Give me a call, and if I can't do it, I'll have one of the ladies from the church swing by and pick you up. There are several that live close by."

Mary's smile faded, but she wasn't going to give up that easily. "Sure, whatever is convenient for you. I'd still love to go back to church. I guess I'll see you at the hospital in a couple of days. I have tomorrow and Tuesday off."

"Sure thing. See you around," Marc said as he walked back to the car and got in. Turning to Aunt Nettie, he said, "Now just what were you trying to pull back there?"

"What do you mean, dear?" Aunt Nettie said.

"You know exactly what I mean. I'm not interested in Mary Landers."

"Well, I'm glad to hear you say it!" Aunt Nettie said firmly.

"You were trying to throw us together. Why are you glad I'm not interested in her?"

"Because she isn't your type, Marc, but I wasn't so sure you knew that. So I sort of tested the water, so to speak. I wanted to give you a chance to be alone with her if you wanted to, but you passed the test, dear, so you can rest your mind." Aunt Nettie reached over and patted him on the cheek just like she used to do when he was little.

Marc shook his head. "I can't believe you. Here you've been pushing me and pushing me to date again. And if you think I might be interested in Mary, you don't want me to really be with her. What gives?"

Aunt Nettie smiled. "Oh, Marc, honey. God's got someone very special picked out for you. It's just that you don't see it right now. But just you wait, when you do see it, you will know that God's timing is just right."

"You really believe that, don't you?" Marc asked incredulously. "What if I don't want anyone? Have you ever taken that into consideration?"

"Oh, phish! You can't really mean that. Melanie was too good of a wife for you to think that."

"Of course, she was a wonderful wife! That's why I'm not replacing her. I can't find anyone that would ever be able to take her place."

"For goodness sake, Marc, you're not replacing Melanie! You could never do that. The woman that God has for you will make her own place in your heart."

"We'll see," Marc said as he pulled into Aunt Nettie's driveway.

"Marc, look at me," Aunt Nettie demanded. When he turned and looked at her, she continued, "Was marriage to Melanie bad or good?"

"You know it was good—no, it was wonderful."

"Then don't you think it would be a compliment to Melanie to want that with someone else? If you would have had a bad marriage, maybe I could see you not wanting to marry again. Because then you would be afraid of getting another bad marriage. But when you have had a good marriage, it would seem like you would want to remarry."

Marc was silent for a while, and then he said, "Okay, Aunt Nettie, I'll tell you what. If that is what God has planned for my life, I won't fight him, but I'm not going out and looking for anyone either."

Aunt Nettie smiled. "Marc, dear, I have a feeling that she's real close even now, but it may take a while before God opens both of your eyes to the fact that you were meant for each other. Don't you worry about it. God is always on time."

"Now who do you have—" Marc started to say.

"Oh, would you look at that! Gertrude Waterman just pulled up to the curb. I would love to carry on this conversation with you, honey, but I really need to get together with Gertrude. We'll talk again some other time," Aunt Nettie said as she scurried from the car and waved to Mrs. Waterman.

Marc knew that she had just dodged his question on purpose, but he planned on asking it again…real soon.

As he backed out of Aunt Nettie's driveway, his eyes fell on the house where Nancy lived. He could see Mark Siders car out front, so he knew that they were all having Sunday dinner. Suddenly he felt very alone. He was going home to an empty house, and there would be no Sunday dinner waiting for him.

Chapter 12

The sun shining into Nancy's window woke her up the next morning. She stretched slowly, enjoying a few minutes of peace and quiet before getting up and getting ready to head out to look for work.

Susan didn't have to work today, so she was going to watch Sarah for her while she spent the morning looking for a job. Hopefully, this day would bring about a change in her circumstances, and she would be able to get a good-paying job. Right now, she would take just about any job she could get.

Getting up and getting dressed, she made her way into the kitchen and found a note from Susan, which read, "I've taken Sarah, and we are going to the park for the morning. I wanted you to get some more rest before your job search. We'll see you when you get back. The keys to my car are on the coffee table. God bless you with a job! We'll be praying."

Nancy smiled as she read the note. She had argued with Susan a little last night about taking her car, but Susan had been right, she needed the car to get around in so that she could apply at more places. She had read the newspaper last night and circle five or six places that had "help wanted" ads.

Grabbing a cup of coffee, she walked through the living room and picked up the keys to the car. Closing her eyes just for a moment, almost as if by habit, she said, "God, you know I really need to find a job…so please will you help me?"

It seemed a bit awkward praying again, but after going to church yesterday and hearing the sermon on faith and that God never lets anyone down, it pricked something inside of Nancy to maybe give

God another chance. After all, maybe God really did care about her…and if not her, he certainly cared about Sarah.

Feeling better about the day, she got into the car and headed downtown where most of the jobs were that were in the newspaper. She knew that most of them were lower-paying jobs, but she didn't really have any experience in anything, except being a secretary in a bank before she met and married Joe. That was a long time ago, and she hadn't worked after getting married. Her lack of recent experience bothered her, but hopefully it wouldn't bother the places where she was going today to put in her applications.

It was a long day for Nancy, by the time she was done, it was three o'clock in the afternoon, and she hadn't had any success. She had gotten to put her application in at only two places because the rest of them had said the job was filled. One place told her that they had twenty applications, but that they would take hers anyway.

Tired and discouraged, Nancy pulled into Susan's driveway. Turning the car off and grabbing her purse, she made her way into the cool interior of the house just as she heard Sarah yell, "Mommy's home!"

Nancy put a smile on her face as her daughter flew out of the kitchen with flour all over her dress and a streak across her nose. "Mommy, Auntie Susan and I are baking some cookies, and they're yummy. I missed you. Did you get a job?"

She looked up from hugging Sarah as Susan said, "Give your mom a little rest, princess. She just got home." Speaking to Nancy, she said, "Come on in the kitchen, and I'll get you some iced tea. You look like you've had a long day."

"Iced tea sounds good, but if I'm going to taste some of those yummy cookies that Sarah made, I'll have to have a glass of milk instead," Nancy said as she smiled down at her daughter.

"They are really yummy, Mommy. Auntie Susan let me have a teensy-weensy taste of one, then she said I could have two of them when you got home. I'm glad you're home!"

Both women laughed as Sarah ran back into the kitchen. Nancy said, "Well, now I know where I rate…right behind the cookies!"

Setting down at the table, all three of them were enjoying the sugar cookies when the phone rang. Susan got up and answered it, then said, "Yes, sir, she's right here. May I ask whose calling?" She listened for a moment and then said, "Oh, hey, Todd, how are you? Great, glad to hear it! Just a minute, and I'll get Nancy on the phone. I'm making cookies, and they need to come out of the oven."

She handed the phone to Nancy and said, "It's the police department."

"Hello?" Nancy said into the phone. "This is Nancy Blackwell speaking."

"Hello, Mrs. Blackwell. I'm Todd Stevens with the Crestmont City Police Department. I was wondering if I could come over this evening and talk with you and your sister. We have picked up a person of interest in the hit-and-run case on your daughter. I would also like to talk to Dr. Marc Carter since he was there at the time of the accident."

"You're welcome to come over, Officer Stevens, any time this evening, but I don't know about Dr. Carter," Nancy replied.

The voice on the other end of the line replied, "I took the liberty of calling Marc a few minutes ago and asking him if I could meet with him. I got him on his cell phone, and he is at his aunt's house… which I believe is just a few houses down from yours. Would it be all right if he came over there, and we could all talk together?"

"I…I guess so. I mean, I don't see what Dr. Carter could have to do with this case."

"He was there at the time of the accident, Mrs. Blackwell, and he was also the attending physician to your daughter. It would be helpful to know if he saw anything at all."

"That is fine. I just don't want to inconvenience the doctor. What time do you want to come over?"

"Would about thirty minutes be too soon?" the officer asked.

"Just a moment, I live with my sister. Let me make sure it is okay with her first." Nancy held her hand over the receiver and asked Susan. At her nod, she spoke back into the phone. "That would be fine. I'll see you in a half hour."

Officer Stevens spoke once more, "Tell Susan that I hope she's making some more of her sugar cookies...all the guys love them around here."

"I'll let her know," Nancy said as she said goodbye and hung up the phone.

"Officer Stevens said he hopes you're making sugar cookies because the men at the station love them."

Susan laughed. "Those guys down there will eat anything sweet! I've made cookies a couple of times and took them down there. The ladies in the church get together once a month and have a big cookie bake. They divide them up and take them to the police station, the fire station, and the city hall. Todd always asked that some of my sugar cookies are in the bunch that the police station gets."

"Boy, you sound popular! Are you sure that you've only got the pastor on your fishing line?"

"Nope, Mark is the only man in my life. I've dated a few guys off and on. In fact, I even went out with Todd a couple of times. That's how come he knows about my sugar cookies, but Todd and I are just friends. Our dates were nothing more than two people who didn't have anything to do, so we decided to do something fun together. We ended up friends."

Nancy finished off her glass of milk and sat it down. Sarah had just finished her second cookie and milk, and she said, "Mommy, is there a policeman coming over here? He won't take you to jail, will he?"

"No, honey, nobody is taking me to jail."

"I 'member that policeman who took daddy to jail that time he hit you," Sarah said innocently.

"Sarah!" Nancy said sharply as she saw Susan turn around and stare at her.

Sarah's little hand went over her mouth, and tears came to her eyes as she said, "I'm sorry, Mommy, I didn't mean to break my promise. You told me not to say anything, and I promised...I...I'm sorry."

Sarah ran to her mother and buried her face into her lap and cried. Nancy smoothed her blond hair and said, "Shhh, honey, it's okay. Don't worry about it."

"But...will Jesus be mad at me for b...breaking my promise?" Sarah looked up at her mom with tears still streaming down her cheeks.

Susan spoke up before Nancy could say anything, "Of course, he won't, princess! Jesus doesn't get mad at us and never forgive us. We always make mistakes, but he loves us so much that he forgives us. I tell you what, how about if you go get ready to take a nice bubble bath with all your toys and get that flour off you before the policeman gets here. You'll feel a lot better, and you'll be as pretty as a picture."

Susan knew that Sarah loved taking bubble baths with all her dolls in the tub that she was allowed to have. Susan had bought her a new rubber doll just a few days ago that Sarah could take in the water with her.

Sarah's face lit up, and her tears stopped flowing, "Okay, Auntie Susan, can I take Dolly in the tub with me?"

"That's what I bought her for. Now scoot...and I'll get the water running for you."

After a few minutes, Susan came back and sat down at the table across from Nancy. "How many times did Joe hit you?"

"Too many times to count," Nancy said, looking down at the crumbs on her plate. "But the night that Sarah is talking about was a bad one. I didn't know that Sarah was awake, he hit me, and I fell against the door, banging my head. Sarah saw it and screamed. It must have been the scream that alerted the neighbors, and they called the police. When the police got there, they saw the blood where I had hit the door, and it was all they needed to take Joe to jail. Sarah and I had two peaceful days until he got out. He didn't hit me again for a while, but then he would get drunk and—"

The doorbell rang, and Nancy jumped at the sound. She had been remembering the bad things, and she didn't like to think about them.

Susan got up and said, "We're not through talking about this, but I want you to tell me when you feel like it. I don't want you to feel like you *have* to tell me." She turned and answered the door. "Hi,

Todd. Hi, Marc, come on in. Nancy's in the kitchen, and I've got sugar cookies made."

Todd spoke up, "I was hoping you'd say those magic words."

They all laughed and made their way into the kitchen. Nancy had quickly schooled her features into a mask. She didn't want anyone to see how the old memories still hurt her so much.

Getting up, she held out her hand to Todd. "Hello, Officer Stevens, I'm Nancy Blackwell."

Todd shook her hand and said, "It's nice to meet you, but just call me Todd. This is a small town, and if I was called Officer Stevens, nobody would know who you were talking about."

Turning to Marc, she said, "Hello, Dr. Carter."

"You've known me longer than Todd…why not call me Marc?"

Susan spoke up, "Now that we've settled the issue of names, let's all sit down and have some cookies."

Nancy said, "I've had enough, but make sure that these two get their share."

"Hey, Susan, do you have any coffee made by chance?" Todd asked, stuffing a cookie in his mouth."

"Hmmm, it just so happens that I put on a pot when I heard you were coming. I know you and your cookies and coffee." Susan pour both Todd and Marc a cup of black coffee, and then they all sat at the table.

When Todd was finished, he pulled out a small notebook from his pocket and then said, "Nancy, do you remember anything at all about the car that hit your daughter? Could you tell me exactly what you saw?"

Nancy thought back to that horrible day, but she had to be honest, all she saw was her daughter being hit by the car and crumpling to the pavement. Her whole focus had been on Sarah. When she mentioned this, Todd nodded. "I understand. This happens a lot of times. It's called tunnel vision. Your mind blocks out everything else around you except what is directly in front of you."

Susan spoke up, "Well, she might not have got a good look at the car, but I did!" She went on to explain exactly what she saw. She had even caught a glimpse of the driver, who had dark-brown hair and a beard. He had on sunglasses because she saw the glint of them when he had turned the corner and drove away.

"Well, we found the car, and we got the owner's name, but the guy claims he had loaned the car to a friend for a week and just got it back. Do you think you could pick this guy out if I showed you some pictures?"

He opened a folder and laid out five pictures. All the men in the pictures had dark hair and a couple of them had beards. Susan shook her head. "I can't really say. These two here look like they could fit the description."

Marc leaned over and looked at the pictures and then said, "I don't know for sure, but this guy right here looks like the guy I saw driving the car. I got a pretty good look at him because he was coming right at me before he swerved and hit Sarah."

"That's pretty interesting because you just picked out the guy that owns the car," Todd said as he put the pictures back in the file.

"So what happens next?" Nancy asked.

"We will file formal charges against him, he'll get a lawyer, and there will be a court hearing. You will all need to be at the hearing."

"Will Sarah need to be there? I really don't want her to if she doesn't have to be."

"I don't think she'll have to be there since we have eyewitnesses to the accident, but we will see how it goes." Todd looked at Susan. Could I beg another one of those cookies from you before I leave?"

"Sure can, and I'll even make up a bag for you to take back to the station...for evidence you know!"

"I can't have that kind of evidence lying around there. I may just have to destroy it all before I get there."

They all laughed, and then Marc said, "Nancy, did you have any luck with your job search today?"

Nancy shook her head. "Not much, I'm afraid. Most of the jobs had already been filled, and the ones that hadn't had lots of applicants. It's been a very frustrating day."

"What kind of job are you looking for?" Todd asked.

"Just about anything really, but I've had experience as a secretary before I got married. Although I didn't work after I was married."

"Are you still married?" Todd asked, glancing down at her ringless hand.

"No, my husband has been dead for almost two years now." Nancy didn't go into any more details.

Todd looked at Nancy Blackwell and liked what he saw. Nancy seemed to be a very good woman, and he could see that she was an extremely attractive one! Her blond hair was sort of long but styled in a way that complimented her face and caused her blue eyes to look even wider and bluer.

He spoke up, "Hey, I just remembered! Beth, our office manager, is leaving next week on maternity leave, and we haven't found a replacement. It makes it hard because she's not sure if she's coming back or not. She'll be gone at least twelve weeks, maybe longer. We need someone to take her place."

Nancy looked interested. "What does she do?"

"Mostly takes care of us guys, keeps us in order, and makes sure our paperwork is done right before she sends it into the state. She does a lot, but you said you were a secretary before. Where were you a secretary?"

"I held a banking position. I took care of most of the paperwork for loans and kept the office running smoothly…or at least I tried to."

"You sound just like someone we need. Why don't you come down to the station tomorrow around ten o'clock, and I'll introduce you to Beth. She's the one who would be hiring her replacement, and she's kinda getting desperate."

Marc watched this exchange, and he saw the way that Todd was looking at Nancy, and he didn't know why, but he didn't like it. It would be good for Nancy to get a job, but did she have to get one where she would be around a man like Todd Stevens? He liked Todd, but he knew for a fact that Todd like to date a lot of women, and he would never pass up an opportunity to date one as pretty as Nancy.

When did he start thinking about how pretty Nancy was? Marc chided himself. He was a married man, he shouldn't be, but then he remembered he wasn't married anymore. And if he was truthful with himself, he found Nancy Blackwell more than just attractive, he found her beautiful. And he didn't like Todd Stevens getting a chance to be around her a lot. Maybe he could find her a job…yeah, that's what he would do, and he'd find her a job at the hospital or… or maybe somewhere closer.

Chapter 13

The next morning, Susan was up early. She got the coffee brewing and was starting to fix breakfast when the phone rang.

"Hello?"

"Hi, is this Susan?" a male voice replied on the other end of the line.

"Yes, it is."

"Hi, Susan, this is Marc. I didn't wake you up, did I?"

"No, I've been up for a while, Dr. Carter. What can I do for you?"

"Is Nancy up?"

"Yes, she is, but she's in the shower right now. Can I give her a message for you?"

"Well, I wanted to talk to her about a job opening I have available in my office. I think it would be a great opportunity for her, and I really need the position filled."

"I see," Susan said. "What position would it be?"

"It's a receptionist, secretary position. And since Nancy has experience in that sort of thing, I figured she might be interested."

"Did Betty quit?" Susan questioned. She had known Dr. Carter's receptionist for a long time, and she didn't figure that Betty would retire early, although she was probably old enough to.

"No, Betty didn't retire, but she is getting older, and my office has grown quite a bit. I have been thinking about hiring someone else to help out, and this seemed like the perfect opportunity."

"I'll let Nancy know as soon as she gets done. She's getting ready to apply down at the police station, you know."

"Ah…yeah, I know. I heard Todd tell her about the position yesterday, but I don't think she would really like working around all of the stuff that goes on there." Marc then added quickly, "Of course, I don't really know. She…ah…she might like that sort of thing, but anyway just have her call my number."

After Susan got his number, she hung up with a grin on her face. She stood for a few minutes looking at the private cell phone number of Marc Carter. She didn't know if Nancy realized it, but Dr. Carter never gave his cell phone number out to anyone…except maybe his aunt. He was a very private person and preferred to keep his cell phone for emergencies only.

Susan thought, *You know, for someone who says she doesn't want to get married again and for a doctor who's afraid of getting married again, this sure sounds strange.* Giggling a little to herself, she laid the phone number on the table where Nancy always sat to drink her coffee. *This is sure going to get interesting around here!*

She poured herself a cup of coffee and, as she heard Nancy emerge from the bathroom, reached for another cup.

Nancy walked into the kitchen and said, "Umm, that coffee smells so good this early in the morning."

"Got you a cup ready right here, and I thought I'd cook you a little breakfast before you go." Susan smiled, sitting the coffee cup down right beside the phone number.

Nancy reached for the cup, noticing for the first time the piece of paper on the table. "What's this?" she asked.

"It's someone that called and wanted to talk to you about a job," Susan said.

"Really!" Nancy said excitedly. "It must have been someone from all the applications that I put in. I can't believe it…I have two job offers now!"

"You don't know the half of it," Susan said under her breath.

"Did you say something?" Nancy said, glancing from the number to Susan smiling by the stove.

"Well, this one is sort of different. You are supposed to call before you leave to go do the other job interview at the police station."

"How did anyone know I was going for an interview this morning?" Nancy asked, completely puzzled.

"It's Marc Carter, Nancy. He wants you to come to his office and interview for a position there."

"Dr. Carter? Now how in the world would I work at his office? I'm not a nurse and have no such training."

"He doesn't need a nurse. He says he needs a receptionist/secretary combined," Susan responded. But to herself, she thought, *What he really needs is a wife!*

"Anyway he heard you say you had experience in doing that sort of thing, so he wants to interview you."

"Well, I have already promised Officer Stevens that I would be down there at two o'clock." Glancing at her watch, she could see she still had over six hours before she had to be there.

"Just go ahead and call and see what he says. It wouldn't hurt because you might not get the job at the police station, or you might not even like it."

Hesitantly Nancy said, "All right, I guess I will. It would be nice to have a choice instead of having to take something I didn't like."

She got up from the table and dialed the number that Susan had given to her, not realizing it was a cell phone. She was surprised when Marc answered. He must really need a receptionist if he's answering his own office phone, she thought.

"Hello, Dr. Carter, this is Nancy Blackwell."

"Hello, Nancy, how are you? I see you got my message."

"Yes, Susan said you had a position that you need to fill in your office."

"Yes, my office has grown, and I need to add some additional help. I have a receptionist who has been with me for a long time. Her name is Betty, but she can't carry the load since I am taking on another neurosurgeon. Would you be interested in the job?"

"Well, it does sound interesting. Could I come in and talk to you in the office and look around? Besides, you don't know if I can do the work, so maybe if I were there, you could tell me what was required, and I could let you know what I can do."

Marc could have kicked himself. He never hired anyone unless they met with him first, and he had never offered a job to anyone before finding out if they could even do it! *Good grief, man, get a grip*, he told himself and then answered, "Yes, of course, you would want to look things over. I've just been in such a hurry lately that I really haven't put much thought into hiring anyone. But when you mentioned that you were looking for work and what you had done before, I just thought it would be a good time to fill the position." He knew he was rattling on, but he didn't know what to say now that he had almost dropped the job in her lap, so to speak.

Nancy glanced at her watch and said, "Would eleven o'clock be okay with you?"

"Sure, that would be fine," Marc said. "I'll see you in my office at eleven."

Nancy hung up the phone and turned to her sister. "That was the strangest job interview I've ever done."

"Why is that?" Susan said as she finished up the pancakes and sat two places at the table. "Did he already give you the job?"

"It sounded like it, but he doesn't even know if I can do the job." Nancy suddenly looked over at Susan suspiciously. "Does this have anything to do with you?"

Susan shook her head. "Not me, this time. I was as surprised as you when I got the phone call this morning."

Nancy sat down at the table and said, "Well, he had better not be doing this out of pity for me! I can work. I know how to hold down a job and work hard." She waited until Susan said grace before continuing, "That's one thing I won't stand for, and I will not be made a welfare case."

"Calm down, Nancy. I don't think Dr. Carter is doing this for any of those reasons. Have you ever considered that he really might need you there?"

"Well," Nancy said as she stabbed a piece of pancake on the end of her fork, "I would only work there if I could actually be doing something he needed."

Susan smiled and said, "Of course, why else would he want you there?"

Nancy glanced over at her sister, but Susan had downed her head and was taking a bite of pancake that was dripping with syrup. When she did look up again, there was total innocence was in her eyes.

Nancy finished getting ready as Sarah sat on the bed still in her pink princess nightgown. "Where are you going, Mommy?"

"I've got to go see about getting a job, sweetie. Dr. Carter called and asked me to come to his office. There might be a job for me there."

"Dr. Angel might have a job for you?" Sarah asked excitedly. "Dr. Angel's office would be a special place to work, you know."

"Why's that, sweetie?"

"'Cause, wherever angels are, that is where God is," Sarah said bluntly.

Nancy looked at her daughter in wonder. She was so young to be thinking about angels and God, and yet here she was talking as if she knew them all personally.

"Well, I don't know about that, but I know that sick people go there, and Dr. Carter tries to help them get well," Nancy said, finishing up the final touches on her hair.

Turning toward her daughter, she said, "Okay, princess, how does Mommy look?"

"Good enough to eat!" Sarah said with enthusiasm. It was a game that they had played often in the past. Nancy would dress Sarah up in the best she had for her and tell her, "You look good enough to eat!" Then she would act like she was gobbling up her belly. It always brought a laugh from Sarah, and now it was Nancy's turn to laugh.

"That's pretty good then, huh?" Nancy said as she tickled Sarah's bare feet.

Screaming and drawing her feet back, she said, "Yes, Mommy, and now that you are going to be working for Dr. Angel, you'll laugh even more."

Nancy sobered up quickly, remembering what Sarah had said the angel had told her. She also realized that she had been laughing more, but it was probably because she was finally getting back on her own two feet.

Sarah reached up and touched Nancy's face. "Mommy, I like it when you laugh. It sounds just like angels singing."

That brought tears to Nancy's eyes. "Sweetheart, I love you. You are so good for Mommy!" She reached out and brought Sarah close to her heart, kissing her gently on the top of her head.

"I love you too, Mommy." Then just as quickly as she started the conversation, Sarah jumped to a new one. "Mommy, do you think I will ever get a new daddy?"

"W…what?" Nancy stammered.

"A new daddy. My old daddy is dead, and he didn't like me. Do you think my new daddy will like me?"

Sarah was asking something that Nancy had no answer for, but a voice from the doorway said, "Princess, if you get a new daddy, he will love you more than anything in the whole world."

"Goody!" Sarah said as she jumped off the bed and ran toward her auntie Susan who stood in the doorway. She grabbed her around the legs and gave her a big hug. "My old daddy died, you know, but he didn't make Mommy laugh. He only made her cry. That made me sad too."

Susan looked up, and Nancy saw the tears that slipped from her eyes. "It made me sad too, princess, but God will take care of you and your mommy now. So he will always give you the best."

Nancy cleared her throat and said, "I've got to go. I told Dr. Carter I would be at his office at eleven."

Susan wiped the tears away and said cheerfully, "Then you'd better scoot! Here's my car key."

Nancy looked at her sister uncertainly. "Are you sure you don't mind me taking your car, and you're watching Sarah again?"

"Look, I don't have to be at work until six this evening. So you've got plenty of time to do what you want."

Nancy smiled gratefully. "It is nice that your schedule has worked out so well for all of us."

"I didn't think I would like the rotating shift, but I do! I've worked this type of shift for almost a year now, and I like it. The one thing I am really thankful for is I don't have to work any graveyard shifts!"

"What's a grabeyard ship?" Sarah asked.

Nancy laughed and said, "I'm leaving. You explain it to her."

As she closed the door, she heard Susan say, "Well, Sarah, it's not a grabeyard ship, it's…"

Getting into the car, she drove toward the office of Marc Carter, wondering what the day held for her and thankful that she was finally going to get a job!

Chapter 14

Nancy walked through the double doors and into the office of Dr. Marc Carter. Walking up to the counter that sat in the middle of the room, she spoke to the older woman behind the desk.

"Hello, my name is Nancy Blackwell. I'm supposed to see Dr. Carter at eleven."

The woman glanced up over her reading glasses and smiled. "Do you have an appointment, Ms. Blackwell?"

"No...I mean...yes, I'm supposed to interview for a job with Dr. Carter."

"Just a moment, and I'll tell him you're here. Go ahead and have a seat. I'm sure Marc will be with you shortly."

Nancy watched as the woman went to the back and turned the corner. Walking over to a bank of chairs, she sat down and picked up a magazine. Flipping through it, nothing really registered on her mind, except the coming interview.

Why had Marc Carter just suddenly called? She glanced around the office and noticed the efficient-looking file cabinets, the phone system, and the receptionist desk. Nowhere she looked did she see a place that could be for a secretary, and it puzzled her. If Marc really needed a secretary, surely he would have a desk and a computer at the very least somewhere around.

"Hello, Nancy, I'm glad you could make it." A male voice spoke up.

Startled, Nancy stood up quickly, almost bumping into Marc as he stood in front of her. Reaching out he placed his hand on her elbow to steady her.

"Oh, goodness, you startled me," Nancy said, wanting to back away from the very male presence that she felt radiating from him, but she couldn't because the chair was right behind her.

Dropping his hand from her elbow, Marc stepped back. He noticed that Nancy seemed nervous, which was unusual from what he had ever seen of her.

"Sorry, about that. Are you ready to look around?" Marc said as he glanced toward his receptionist Betty Ward. "I think you've already met Betty. She's been with me for almost as long as I've had a practice here in town…which is a long time. She keeps all of my patients straight."

Betty walked over and held out her hand. "It's so good to meet you, dear. I've heard a lot about you already."

"You have?" Nancy was puzzled. Why would Marc talk about her to his receptionist?

"Oh yes, Marc's aunt and I are close friends. We see each other at least once a week unless one of us is sick. She told me that she had met you and your darling little girl. I would love to meet your daughter myself someday," Betty said.

"Oh, I see. Yes, Mrs. Matthews is a wonderful lady. Sarah… that's my daughter…has already taken to calling her auntie Nettie, and she loves her dog."

Betty laughed. "I gave Nettie that dog about twelve years ago. I can hardly believe he is still alive, but she loves him like a child, and he's been a good companion for her too."

Marc shuffled his feet a little and then cleared his throat. "Ah… if it would be all right, I'd like to show you the rest of the office."

Betty spoke up, "Well, for goodness sake, here I am taking up all your time. We'll talk some more again later, dear."

"I'd like that," Nancy said with a smile as she followed Marc down the hallway and into the back part of his office.

He showed her the three examination rooms, the copier room, and the break room. Then he took her into his office and closed the door. Walking over to his desk, he motioned for her to take a seat.

Nancy sat down in a burgundy leather chair in front of his massive desk. Looking around, she noticed that the desk was filled with paperwork. There were three piles on the corner and another bunch haphazardly scattered around the desk.

Marc spoke up, "As you can see, I'm not very organized when it comes to my office." He spread his hands over his desk. "I'm just too busy with patients to take care of the paperwork. Betty has been doing as much as she can, but she can't be in here and manage the receptionist part too."

"What would my duties be, and where would I have a desk?" Nancy asked.

"Well, most of the time, you would be my secretary and keep things in order for me, like clearing off all this paperwork for me. And you would also be taking over for Betty part-time. She wants to cut back to three or four days a week, and I need someone who could fill in for her. As for as where you would be"—he pointed to a closed door off to his left—"there is a small office that is connected to mine. It has a desk and a computer already there. There is also a door that opens up into the reception area. That way you could see if you were needed in there."

Nancy nodded. "That sounds like something I can handle, but you know that I also have an interview later on today. I would like to see how that one goes also." She didn't want to make any commitments right now.

"I completely understand," Marc said and then named an amount that she would be getting for a salary that set her back.

"Are you sure that's the going rate for a secretary? That sounds like a lot of money," Nancy asked, amazed at the large amount.

"I'm sure, at least for this office it is. Believe me, you will earn every penny of it." Marc smiled and then looked at his watch. "I've kept you a long time, and it's almost noon. Why don't I buy you lunch and we'll finish talking about the position? I'm sure you have more questions for me."

Marc realized that Nancy was unsure of going out to eat with him, so he decided to push a little more, "You've got to eat before you go to your next interview. After all, it would be terrible to pass out in the police department."

Nancy smiled, then relented, "All right, you talked me into it."

"Good, I'll let Betty know, and then we can go."

A few minutes later, Marc helped Nancy into his midsize SUV. Nancy was glad the car was parked under a shade tree because the leather seats would have been murder if the car would have been sitting in the hot sun.

Marc got in and started the car, watching carefully behind him as he backed out. Nancy glanced at his strong hands that rested on the steering wheel. It felt odd, but somehow comforting to be riding in a car with Marc Carter. She didn't quite know what to think of her feelings, so she pushed them aside as she said, "Where are we going?"

"I know a small place not too far from here that serves up some great barbeque. I didn't think to ask if you liked Texas style barbeque!"

Nancy laughed and said, "I was born and raised in Texas. How I could not like barbeque? Especially if we're talking brisket!"

"Now that is a true Texan! I wasn't born or raised here, but I got here as quick as I could!" Marc joked back.

"That is spoken like a true transplanted Texan." She was surprised at how easy it was to talk to Marc. "I hated being away from here after I got married."

"Where did you live while you were married? And for how long?" Marc asked as he pulled into an empty parking spot in front of the Texas Gold Barbeque House.

"I lived in Oklahoma, and it was way too long. Oklahoma has it all…tornados, ice storms, snow, wind, rain. I'm just glad to be back home."

They were met at the door by a smiling waitress who showed them to a table by a window. "How are you today, Dr. Carter?" the waitress asked as she placed silverware in front of them.

"I'm fine, Abby, how are you?"

"Fair to middlin'. You know me, Doc, I'm always doing pretty good." Abby, the waitress, replied with a smile. "Now you know how it's done here, so why don't you show your pretty friend the ropes?"

"Will do!" Marc said as he turned to Nancy.

"Come on, and you'll soon be eating the best barbeque in Texas."

Walking up to a long, low counter with slabs of pork, beef, and sausage laying in neat rows. Each bunch had someone standing behind it with a huge fork and knife in their hands.

"Just tell them what you want, and they'll cut it off for you," Marc said. Then looking at one of the men behind the counter, he said, "Hey, Tony, I want some of that brisket and a piece of sausage."

A big African American with a bright smile said, "Sure nuff, Doc. How much you want? We got us some good banana pudd'n for desert so don't you go clogging your arteries with this beef here…you leave room for Mama's pudd'n."

"Man, you know I can't turn down Mama's banana pudding. I'll make sure I save room." Turning to Nancy, he said, "You better save room too. Mama cooks the best banana pudding I have ever tasted."

Nancy nodded and smiled giving Tony her order, but for a much smaller piece of brisket and no sausage. They both made their way around to the other counter, getting helpings of potato salad and baked beans.

They sat back down at their table, and Marc said, "Do you mind if I ask the blessing?"

"No, go right ahead," she said as she bowed her head. She glanced up slightly and thought how good it was to have a man ask the blessing at the table. Joe wouldn't even allow her to pray over their food, although she did it silently anyway. And when Joe wasn't there, she taught Sarah to pray.

Closing her eyes, she remembered the time that Sarah had tried to ask the blessing when Joe was home. He got so mad that he knocked all the food off the table and stormed out of the house. She tried to calm Sarah and pick up the food from the floor at the same time. Never again did Sarah ask to say the blessing when Joe was home. From that point on, she was scared to death of her own father.

Marc cleared his throat. "Ah…are you still blessing your food?"

Nancy realized that her eyes were still shut, she quickly opened them and said, "I'm sorry, it was just some old memories coming back."

"From the frown on your face, I would say they weren't real good ones."

Nancy shook her head. "No...no, they weren't, but let's talk about something more pleasant."

As they ate, Marc told Nancy a little more about his office and how many patients he had. She could tell that he seemed to care about each one as he talked.

Finally, he said, "And of course, there is Sarah...I'm supposed to see her next week, right?"

Nancy nodded. "Yes, I have an appointment for her on Tuesday at ten o'clock. She's already looking forward to seeing her Dr. Angel again."

Marc laughed and shook his head. "I can't believe that she hangs on to that name for me. I've been called a lot of things in my life but never an angel, so this is a first for me."

Marc was having a good time with Nancy. She was easy to talk to, and there seemed to be no lull in the conversation. He had forgotten how good it felt to have a woman sitting across from and sharing a meal with him. He was surprised at how he felt and at the fact that he didn't even feel guilty about it. Maybe Aunt Nettie was right, maybe he was getting over Melanie, and it was time to get on with his life.

Looking at Nancy, he took in her beautiful hair that was done in some type of loose bun or something. He didn't know much about such things, but he knew that he liked how some of the tendrils had come loose and hung in slight curls about her face, framing it even more. The sun was shining on her, and her eyes seemed to light up as she talked. He had never seen her so animated and happy before. The darkness was fading from her eyes, except for that moment when she had first opened her eyes after he had prayed. Something seemed to haunt her, and he had a feeling it had to do with her past marriage.

Nancy glanced at her watch and said, "Oh, goodness, I only have a little while before I have to be at the interview at the police station. I hate to hurry off, I've had such a good time, and the food was wonderful...including the banana pudding!"

Just as they were getting up to leave, a tall, elegant dark-skinned woman walked over to their table, "Doc, how have you been?"

Marc turned and smiled. "Mama, I've been fine as frog's hair."

The woman let out a belt of laughter and said, "I'm gonna get you to talking like a true Southerner yet, Marc Carter, you just wait."

Marc laughed and then said, "Mama, I want you to meet a friend of mine, Nancy Blackwell. Nancy, this is the owner of this place and one of the best cooks in Texas. Her real name is Lucinda Johnson, but everyone calls her Mama."

The dark eyes turned to Nancy, and she said, "That's right, and I expect you to call me the same thing. Any friend of Marc Carter is a friend of Mama's. How was the food?"

Nancy smiled and said, "Delicious, I haven't had good Texas barbeque since I've moved back, so you've made my day. And the banana pudding was out of this world!"

"Well, now you just made my day too, honey. You make sure you come back and see us again. Marc, you better bring her back here, or I'll tan your hide," Mama mockingly threatened.

"Well, if I can talk her into working for me, I'm sure we'll be back," Marc said as he paid the bill, and they left.

Getting back into the car, Nancy said, "When do you need an answer from me?"

"Right now, but I'll wait until tomorrow," Marc teased.

"All right, I will call you and let you know my decision tomorrow after I get through with both interviews, and I've had a chance to think about them."

"I'll be looking forward to hearing from you."

Marc pulled back into his private parking place and got out, walking around to open the door for Nancy. She had been ready to get out on her own because she wasn't use to anyone opening a door for her.

"It was really nice of you to take me to lunch, Dr. Carter," Nancy said as she got out and held out her hand to shake his.

He reached out and took her hand, feeling the velvety smoothness beneath his palm. He held it for as long as was decent, then reluctantly let it go, saying, "It was really my pleasure, but would you please call me Marc? After all, we may be working together."

"If that happens, I'll have to call you Dr. Carter for sure. You'll be my employer!"

"I don't think so. Did you hear what Betty called me? I've never been Dr. Carter to her, and I'm sure she would tell you the same thing."

Nancy smiled and said goodbye, walking toward her car in the parking lot. Marc watched her walk away, noticing how she moved so gracefully. The further away she got, the lonelier he felt. Turning toward his office, he decided the only way he could forget the empty feeling was just to get to work and forget it. But one thing he couldn't forget was the way the softness of Nancy's hand felt in his.

Chapter 15

Driving toward downtown and the police station, Nancy kept remembering how she had such a good time eating with Marc. She also could still feel the strength of his hand on hers. He seemed to be a good, upright, and honest man, and she couldn't help but think he would be a good employer too.

The only problem that she could see was how she felt when she was around him. For some reason, she was usually nervous or… or something. She couldn't explain it exactly, but sometimes she was afraid that she could fall in love with Marc Carter very easily if given the chance.

Falling in love was something that she couldn't and wouldn't do. All falling in love did for a person was cause them to not see the other person's faults and failures. If she would have known what Joe had been like before they had gotten married, then her life would be so much better now…except she wouldn't have Sarah. For Sarah, she would go through it all again; she had been worth all of the pain of her marriage.

But she wouldn't want Sarah to go through the hurt and pain again for anything in this world that was another reason she would never marry. She would never be able to trust another man to treat her daughter right and love her the way she deserved to be loved. Sarah was a wonderful child, and she deserved all of Nancy's love and attention.

After pulling into an open parking space beside the police department, Nancy checked her hair, smoothing it down where the wind had blown it a little. She wanted to make a good impression here because she wanted to have a choice of jobs.

She remembered Joe telling her over and over how worthless she was whenever she mentioned going back to work. He would sneer at her and say, "You can't go back to work. All you ever did was sit behind a desk and file a few papers. Nobody is looking for an uneducated, lazy person like you to work for them. So give it up, Nancy, you'll never find anybody that would even want to hire you."

"But Joe isn't here anymore," Nancy said out loud as she opened the door of the car. Even so, the memories of his put-downs were still there, making her feel almost worthless. Then she remembered Sarah again, and she squared her shoulders and walked into the building. She could do anything she put her mind to!

Going to the window in the front of the first office, she gave her name and told them why she was there. In just a couple of minutes, Todd Stevens opened a side door and said, "Hello, Nancy, it's good to see you again. Come on back to my office, and we'll talk."

Nancy nervously shifted her purse from her right hand to her left and followed Todd back to his office. He motioned for her to take a seat as he sat down in the chair behind the desk.

"So tell me what you've done as far as a secretarial position before," Todd began.

"Well, it's been a few years since I've done any work actually. I've been a stay-at-home mom since Sarah was born. And since my husband died about two years ago, I haven't worked either. But now that Sarah and I are trying to get settled, I've got to get a job."

"Our secretary has one more week before she leaves to take another job, and she is the one that is really going to be doing the hiring. She knows more about the job than I do. She's out of the office right now but should be back at any time. I just wanted to have a chance to talk to you again."

Nancy heard the interest in his voice and felt his direct gaze on her as she nervously fiddled with her purse. What made her feel so nervous around Todd? Although she had felt nervous around Marc, it wasn't an uneasy nervousness like it was now. Some inner warning signal seemed to be going off in her brain as she sat there.

God, if this isn't the job for me, I want you to not let me get this job, Nancy found herself nervously praying, something she hadn't done in a long time.

A knock on the office door sounded, and the door opened a bit. A man stuck his head in and said, "Serena is back now and wants to go ahead with the interview for the office manager position."

"Okay, I'll bring Nancy down there in just a couple of minutes," Todd said with a slight edge to his voice.

The man nodded and closed the door. Todd waited a few moments and then said, "Look, Nancy, don't let Serena bully you around. She's like that, and she hasn't hired one person in all the people that she's seen. She knows she's leaving in a week, and she doesn't have much time. I don't know what her hold up is, but to me, she's being really stupid. But then what can you expect from someone like...well, never mind. Just don't let her push you around."

Nancy didn't know how to respond, but the word *stupid* stuck in her mind, bouncing around inside like a rubber ball. As she walked down the hall with Todd to another office, the click of her heels seemed to say "stu-pid, stu-pid" over and over.

Just as they reached the office door, Todd stopped her with a hand on her shoulder. "Maybe after the interview, I could take you out to eat or something?"

"I...I don't know. Susan and Sarah will be waiting for me at home. Maybe some other time, okay?" she stammered.

A change happened in his eyes that caused Nancy to blink. It had reminded her so much of Joe and how he looked when she told him she didn't feel like doing something he wanted to do. Once she remembered being sick, and he had wanted to go to a movie. She had asked him if she could just stay home and he could go on to the movie, maybe even take one of his friends. But Joe had gotten so mad that he had backhanded her across the mouth, causing a horrible bruise and had broken one of her teeth. She could almost feel the pain in her jaw as she watched the change come into Todd Stevens's eyes. But as quickly as it happened, it disappeared, leaving her wondering if she had seen it at all.

"Sure, maybe some other time," he said as he opened the door to the secretary's office.

Inside was a petite black-haired woman sitting at a desk, typing on a computer. She glanced up and then frowned when she saw Todd.

"I'll take it from here, Stevens," she said tartly, dismissing Todd quickly.

The woman stood up and smiled at Nancy. "Hello, my name is Serena. I hear you're interested in the secretarial position."

Nancy felt more at ease and said, "It's nice to meet you, Serena, and yes, I'm interested in the position. But to be honest, I haven't worked as a secretary for quite a few years, and I really don't know if I'm qualified."

Serena smiled again and said, "Thanks for being honest. I appreciate that in a person. You don't find much of that in the world we live in today." Changing to a different program on the computer, she said, "Move that chair over there closer so that you can see the computer screen, and I'll go over some things with you, and you can let me know about what you know."

After about thirty minutes of going over different aspects of the police department computer program and what was required, Nancy said, "Serena, let's stop. You have shown me so much that my head is spinning."

Serena gave her a pitying look and said, "I'm sorry, I know I went over things pretty fast. I didn't mean to burden you with everything at once. It's just that things in a police department happen pretty fast, and you have to be prepared to switch gears in midmotion."

"I understand, but I will tell you that I don't think I'm qualified for this position. I've been away from computers for at least five years. I had a computer at home, but it was an outdated one, and I could barely get the Internet up on it, so most of the things that you have showed me is way over my head right now."

"Nancy, I really like you. I think if you learned the programs, you could do the job. You seem to pick up on things pretty quick. Would you like to come back in a few days and go over it again? Maybe then it wouldn't seem so overwhelming to you."

Nancy was surprised to hear Serena say that she seemed to pick up on things quick. It was like healing ointment over the open wounds that Joe left in her heart, but Nancy also knew her limits. "No, I don't think I'm the right person for this job. I don't want to mess up, and the police department doesn't need someone who doesn't know how to do their job." Nancy got her purse and stood up ready to leave.

"I've got to find someone who could do this job." Serena worried over the prospect of not finding anyone yet. "Do you know of anyone that would be able to do this? The pay is excellent, and the hours are really good too."

Nancy's mind went to Susan. "My sister, Susan, isn't looking for another job, but the one she has doesn't pay as well as this one. Let me tell her about it and get back to you. Would that be all right?"

"It would be a lifesaver!" Serena said. "I know Susan, but I didn't know if she would want to work here under some of the conditions." Serena glanced at the door and then back at Nancy, but she didn't say anything.

"Well, I'll ask her, and then if you'll give me your number, I'll call you and let you know."

Serena wrote down her phone number and said goodbye. Nancy walked out of the office and hurried down the hallway, hoping to get away before she saw Todd Stevens again. Just as she was opening the door to exit, Todd called her name.

"Nancy! How did the job interview go? Did you get the job?"

Nancy took a deep breath and turned. "No, I—" She didn't get to finish.

Todd became noticeably upset as he said, "I knew it! I don't understand what is wrong with her. She's leaving in a week, and she's got to find someone. Everybody that's even showed up for this job, something has been wrong with them…I knew she wouldn't hire you either. I'm tired of this. I'm going to talk to her right now."

"Wait, Todd, it's not like that at all. Serena wanted me to take the job, but I don't feel qualified. It's not her fault at all. It's mine," Nancy hurriedly said.

"What do you mean you aren't qualified? All you do is sit in front of the computer all day and fill out a few papers. Any idiot can do it!" Todd was so frustrated that he ran his fingers through his hair, messing up the carefully combed style.

Nancy had had enough. "Then if any idiot can do it, why don't you try!" With that, she turned and walked to her car. "Nancy!" She heard Todd yell behind her, but she didn't stop. She had promised herself after Joe had died that she wasn't going to be anyone doormat anymore, and she had meant it.

Pulling out of the parking lot, she drove away. A sense of peace and relief swept over her, and she seemed to feel the presence of God…something she hadn't felt in a long time…come into the car.

"I prayed, Lord, asking you not to let me get this job if it wasn't your will, and you answered my prayer. Maybe I've been wrong about you all this time. Maybe Sarah's been right—you really do still care about me. I'm sorry, Father. I am asking you to forgive my stubbornness and unbelief and help me to be the kind of mother and woman you want me to be," Nancy prayed all the way home.

As she pulled into the driveway and got out of her car, she heard a voice from down the road, saying, "Yoo-hoo, Nancy, could I talk to you for a minute?"

Nancy looked up and saw Mrs. Matthews waving from her front porch.

"Sure, Mrs. Matthews, I'll be right there."

Walking toward the older woman, Nancy smiled. She liked Mrs. Matthews a lot and being around her always made her feel better.

"Is there something I can do for you?" Nancy said as she got closer.

"Yes, dear, there is. I baked these chocolate chip cookies for Marc, and he just called and told me he couldn't come over tonight. I was so disappointed because he loves chocolate chip cookies. They're his favorite you know."

Nancy smiled. "No, I didn't know that, Mrs. Matthews, but what does that have to do with me?"

"I hope you don't mind me asking, but could you possibly take these over to his house tonight? He likes them fresh, and I made them special. I would hate to see them get stale, and then he wouldn't eat them."

Nancy glanced back at Susan's house, not seeing her or Sarah. "I…I guess I could run them over right now, but why don't I just take you over there, and you can give them to him?"

"Oh no, dear, I can't leave. I'm expecting a phone call from Betty, and I need to talk to her. I'm sure Marc won't mind a bit if you would bring them over. In fact, I'll give him a call when you leave and tell him you're coming. Here I've got a map all drawn out showing you how to get to his house. It's real easy since this is such a small town."

Nancy felt trapped, and there was nothing she could do but take the cookies all wrapped up nice and neat and the piece of paper with a map neatly drawn on it.

"I'll need to check and make sure that Susan and Sarah aren't home yet. They were supposed to be back by now."

"Don't worry about that a bit. I just talked to Susan and that precious little Sarah, and they were going to go to the park. They told me to tell you not to expect them back for at least an hour, and that was only about ten minutes ago. If they come back by before you get back, I'll let them know. In fact, I'll have them come in, and I'll serve them some cookies and milk. I know that Sarah would love that."

Smiling, Nancy agreed and made her way back to her car that was still parked in Susan's driveway. Carefully putting the cookies on the passenger side, she got in and started the car, backing out of the driveway and headed toward Marc Carter's house.

She glanced up to see Mrs. Matthews waving from the front porch with a smile on her face. Nancy waved back and hoped that Mrs. Matthews remembered to call Marc and let him know she was coming.

Chapter 16

Marc was busy; he had been on the phone off and on trying to get through to a doctor from out of state. He had finally reached him and had been talking for over an hour. Now that he had finally hung up, he figured he had better get himself something to eat.

Walking into the kitchen, he frowned. He hadn't been home a lot lately, and when he had been, it was to rush in, grab a microwave dinner or something fast and rush out again. The little bit of dishes that he had used was piled in the sink and in need of being put in the dishwasher.

He rolled up his sleeves and started rinsing the dishes. He glanced out into his backyard and saw that the grass needed cutting again. He should go ahead and hire a landscaper, but he had always enjoyed taking care of his lawn. Of course, that was when Melanie and Amber were still alive, and he had a reason to be home with his family. Now that they were gone, he would just as soon be at work than here with a house full of memories.

Thinking about Melanie always brought a rush of feelings. Most of them were loneliness. He couldn't count the times that he had seen Melanie standing right here at the kitchen sink doing the dishes or cooking. She was always doing something in the kitchen because she loved to cook, but the things she loved most of all was being a mom and be a wife.

Sighing, he put the last glass in the dishwasher, added soap, and turned it on. Looking around the living room, he could see Melanie's presence everywhere he turned from the sofa with its modern curved wood to the matching drapes that hung in the windows.

Sitting down in his recliner, he reached for the paper that he hadn't gotten to read yet. Inside was an insert on different homes that were for sale around the area. One of the pictures caught his eye. It was an older Victorian home that had just been remodeled. Opening the insert, he found an article about it inside.

There were more pictures of the home, taken from just about every angle you could think of. The photographer had even captured the beauty of the grand staircase that graced the entrance way. It was just like a home that he had always wanted.

As he read the article, he saw they were holding an open house all this week. He glanced at his watch and realized they would still be open for over an hour. He would love to go and see it, if only to look.

Grabbing his keys from the coffee table where he always put them, he hurried toward the door and opened it. As he did, he almost plowed into Nancy who was reaching out to ring the doorbell.

"Oh!" Nancy said as she tried to keep the cookies from being dropped.

"Nancy!" Marc said as he reached out and steadied her.

"I…I was bringing over the chocolate chip cookies that your aunt called you about," Nancy replied, holding out the plate but backing away from him a little.

It seemed that whenever she got to close to him, butterflies twisted and turned in her stomach, and she wanted to move closer. She was always disgusted with herself; she knew that she was only being drawn to his masculinity, and that was all…at least that was what she told herself. A niggling little voice in the back of her head said, "Todd Stevens was masculine, and all you wanted to do was run from him."

Pushing that thought aside, she stepped back another step as Marc said, "Aunt Nettie sent these over?"

"Yes, she told me she would call and let you know I was coming…didn't she do that?"

"Well, to be honest, she probably tried, but I've been on the phone ever since I got home. She probably couldn't get through, but I'm always thankful for her chocolate chip cookies! I had called her earlier today to let her know I was going to be busy most of the day.

She told me she was going to make cookies, but I told her I couldn't pick them up. It's just like Aunt Nettie to think of some way to get them to me."

"Well, here you go. I've got to get back home. I'm sure that Susan and Sarah will be getting home soon, and they'll be looking for me."

"Nancy, wait," Marc said as she turned to leave. "Ah, do you have any plans for this evening?"

"No, not really," Nancy said. "I was just planning on going home and taking a long hot bath. It's been a busy day."

"I'd like to hear about your interview at the police station. And I was just on my way over to look at an open house. It's a beautiful Victorian home, and I've always like those type of houses. Would you be interested in going with me? We could grab a bite to eat after we look at the house."

Hesitatingly Nancy replied, "I told your aunt I would be right back, and she was going to relay the message to Susan and Sarah."

"I'll call Aunt Nettie on my cell phone and let her know. Then she can let Susan and Sarah know. Is that okay with you?"

Nancy still hesitated, but she loved old Victorian houses and had always dreamed of one day owning one, even if she had to fix it up herself. Marc had the picture in the paper in his hand; he held it out to her. "Here, this is a picture of the outside."

Nancy looked at it and was awestruck. It was the most perfect home she had ever seen. Looking from the picture to Marc, she replied, "If you'll call, I'll go."

"Let's take my car, and I'll call on the way."

They got into his car that was still sitting in the driveway. Thankfully clouds had moved in, and it had cooled a little. The interior of the car wasn't as hot as it would have normally been, and the air-conditioning was soon making it more comfortable.

Nancy watched the scenery go by as Marc finished calling his aunt. When he snapped his cell phone shut, he said, "Aunt Nettie said all was going good. She had invited Susan and Sarah over to have dinner with her tonight, and they were already there. They had left a note on the door for you to come over when you got back from my house. Aunt Nettie did tell me that she tried to call…she even sounded a little ticked at me because she couldn't get through," he said with a laugh.

"Well, I'm glad she did try to call. I would have felt funny if she had forgotten."

"Aunt Nettie is still really sharp. There isn't much she forgets, and she has never forgotten to call me every day, especially since my wife and daughter passed away."

Nancy was startled; she hadn't known he had been married. She had suspected, but she hadn't known.

"I'm sorry to hear about your wife and daughter…I…I didn't know."

"It will soon be three years. They were in a car wreck together. I don't really like thinking about it much."

"I know what you mean. Joe's been gone for almost that long, and I still can't believe it is real."

Marc glanced over at Nancy and said, "Did you have a good marriage?"

"At first, we did. I fell in love with Joe when I was still young. It was a whirlwind romance, and we were soon married. We didn't have Sarah until we had been married a couple of years."

Marc nodded. "I had known Melanie all of my life, at least it seemed that way. We went to high school together, but I didn't date her then. I went off to college and became a doctor. She stayed here and worked in the library. One day, I came back to visit Aunt Nettie and had to go to the library to work on a thesis for college. That's when I met Melanie again. But this time, she seemed so different, so…I don't know…so grown up. From that time on, we dated when I could come back. As soon as I graduated, she and I got married. We had to move away for a few years so that I could do my internship at a bigger hospital, but I had always known I would come back here and work."

"But you told me that you weren't a Texan."

"Nope, I'm not. I was born in North Dakota. I lived there until I was twelve when my parents passed away. They were killed in a plane crash while going on their second honeymoon. I came to live with Aunt Nettie and finished school here."

Nancy looked over at him and said, "I thought I had a lot of sorrow…but you've had much more than I ever had. How do you do it?"

"How do I do what?" Marc asked puzzled.

"How do you still have your faith in God?"

Marc smiled. "I can thank Aunt Nettie for most of it. She was there for me. She was my dad's sister, and she took me in immediately after the funeral. I was not a happy camper when I first came to live with her. I had just lost my parents and had moved thousands of miles from all of my friends. I figured that God had let me down, even though my parents had taken me to church all of my twelve years."

"But what changed your thinking?" Nancy was puzzled. Even though she was slowly coming around to see that God really cared about her, she still didn't have the faith that Marc had.

"Aunt Nettie changed my thinking. I was pretty bad for a while, and I guess I sort of took it all out on poor Aunt Nettie. Uncle Charlie had already passed away, so she was raising me on her own. I was ranting at her one day, upset because of something that happened at school, when all of a sudden, I said, 'What do you know about anything? You've never lost someone you love!' Boy, did that ever get me in trouble. It was the only time I remember Aunt Nettie being really upset at me."

"I can't imagine Nettie Matthews getting upset at anything."

"Believe it! She told me, 'So you think you're the only one who's ever lost a parent or someone you love? You don't even know what you're talking about. Did you ever stop to think that your daddy was my brother? I loved him like a son! Our mother and daddy…your grandpa and grandma Carter…died when I was sixteen, and your daddy was thirteen. I raised your daddy and watched him grow up. Now he has passed on before me. That's when I tried to say something, but she kept talking. 'And let me tell you something else. I lost my husband, your uncle Charlie, before you were ever born. So, young man, don't you ever tell me that I don't know what it's like to lose someone I loved.' With that, she turned and marched away.

"I just stood there, not knowing what to say. Then I heard a sound coming from Aunt Nettie's bedroom. She had went in there and thought she had shut the door, but it was open just enough for me to see her though the crack. She was kneeling beside her bed, and she was crying."

"Oh my! What did you do?"

"I just stood there and listened as I cried with her. She was praying, and she was asking God to help her raise me in the right way. To raise me to believe in him and to love him no matter what happened. And what got to me the most was that she asked God to help her not to get bitter anymore about all of her loved ones going to heaven without her. When she said that, I realized that Aunt Nettie had fought hard to overcome the bitterness that gets into your soul when you lose someone close to you or if God doesn't do exactly what you want him too."

Nancy tried to swallow the lump that rose up in her throat as she thought about the little boy and Nettie Matthews overcoming so much loss when she couldn't seem to get over her ruined marriage and the loss of a husband that she had almost come to hate.

She closed her eyes for a few seconds and breathed a prayer for help. Help to become the kind of woman that Nettie Matthews was and help to raise Sarah in the love of God. She determined then and there that she would continue to go to church and get back with the God that she had left behind.

Soon they saw the signs that pointed the way to the Victorian home. Turning into a tree-lined driveway, they wound back and forth until suddenly before them, on a slight hill, was a beautiful eighteenth-century Victorian home. It sat like a beautiful southern belle on the hill. The house was painted a soft delicate yellow with blue and white trim.

"Oh, Marc, it's beautiful!" Nancy breathed.

"Yeah, I sort of feel the same way," Marc said as he sat for a few minutes just looking at the house.

"Let's go in and see if it's as pretty on the inside as it is on the outside," he added.

Getting out of the car, they walked up the front steps and stepped onto the open porch. The door was open, and a woman greeted them, "Hello, my name is Wilma Moore. Welcome to our open house."

"Hello, Ms. Moore. My name is Marc Carter, and this is…" he started to introduce Nancy when Wilma said,

"Dr. Marc Carter?"

"Yes, I'm a doctor."

"I've heard about you, Doctor!" the woman gushed and then shook hands with Nancy. "And this must be Mrs. Carter. It is a pleasure to meet you!"

"But I'm not—" Nancy tried to say.

"Now come on in and let me show you around!" Wilma Moore wasn't letting any grass grow under her feet, and she wasn't letting anyone else say a word.

Marc and Nancy looked at each other, and both shrugged their shoulders…they had both tried. Instead they followed Ms. Moore around the home as she showed them all of the features of the downstairs. The formal dining room, the sitting room, the living room, and then the huge kitchen with every modern appliance available.

"Now let's go upstairs. You will just die when you see the layout!"

Following her to the second floor, they found five more bedrooms and three baths upstairs. Walking into the biggest bedroom, Ms. Moore said, "Now this is the master bedroom with every convenience you can name. I'm sure you will love the huge bathroom… plenty of room for two people! And then the huge walk-in closet, which I'm sure Mrs. Carter has plenty of lovely dresses to put into this one!"

Nancy almost laughed out loud as she thought of her meager belongings, which included exactly two dresses! They would look lost in the closet that was bigger than her entire bedroom that she shared with Sarah.

"Oh, and here is the best feature of all!" the woman continued to gush as she flung open a door that was connected to the master bedroom.

They stepped inside, and there Nancy saw a room that was designed for a princess! Wouldn't Sarah love this, she thought as she looked around. It was done in pink with white floating clouds all over the ceiling. The soft pink gave way to white wainscoting below.

"Wouldn't Sarah love this room!" Nancy said without thinking.

"Oh, so you have a daughter?" the woman asked.

"Yes, she's five, and she loves princess stuff," Nancy acknowledged.

"Is she your only one?" asked the woman again. At Nancy's nod, the woman started in again, "Because I was going to say that if you had a son, this room can easily be repainted into a blue…it was painted for the McFarland's little girl, but they've moved back to Spain, and they are anxious to sell…you two seem like the perfect family for a home like this…with plenty of growing room for an expanding family!"

Nancy turned red and looked down at her flat stomach, thinking, "Do I look pregnant?" She glanced up at Marc, and as he shook his head know, her face flamed even brighter when she realized he knew what she was thinking.

"Well, thank you, Ms. Moore, for showing us the house. It is beautiful, and Nancy and I will talk it over. This is the first house we've looked at, so we will have to get back to you," Marc said as he took Nancy's hand and led her out to the car.

After getting into the car, Nancy said, "Why didn't you tell her we weren't…you know…married?"

"And break the woman's heart? She was so set on us having that house. It would have crushed her if we would have told her the truth. How can you be so heartless?" Marc teased.

"But…but…she thought…" Nancy sputtered.

"She thought we would want to have more children. She didn't think that you were pregnant, so don't worry," Marc replied with a grin.

Nancy blushed again and turned her head away from him. He was very close in the car, and she could feel him beside her, even if she didn't look at him. What would it be like to be married to a man who liked to tease? A man who was so kind and considerate? Nancy sighed. She had had her chance, and now she would never know.

Chapter 17

As they drove back among the oak trees that lined the driveway, Marc turned and glanced at Nancy, then asked, "You never did tell me about your interview with the police department. How did it go?"

Nancy hesitated; she didn't want him thinking that she was throwing the job interview at the police department simply because she wanted to work for him, and she couldn't tell him about Todd and how she felt around him.

"It went all right, I guess. The woman who interviewed me was named Serena."

"Serena Osgood?" Marc asked.

"I don't know her last name, she never said, but she was a really nice woman. I think she really wanted me to take the job."

"And…?"

"And…well, I can't. I just don't feel like it is where I should be. I…well, let's just say I don't feel real comfortable there."

Marc smiled and said, "So does that mean that you're coming to work for me?"

Again, she hesitated before answering, "I don't know, Marc. Don't get me wrong. I really appreciate the job offer…"

"Then why aren't you taking it?"

Nancy blushed. How was she supposed to tell him that she was worried about being around him all the time? That wasn't something you just blurted out…and if she did, Marc would probably take it the wrong way.

"Well, I just think that I need a few days to think about it, that's all," Nancy said instead.

"I tell you what, why don't you come in for just a few days and see how you do? If it doesn't work out, if you don't feel right about being there, then you can find another job," Marc insisted.

"But what would Betty think? After all, she would have to train me to do her job, and she would be spending all of that time on me, and then if I up and quit, it would be wasted."

"Betty would enjoy the company, I assure you. I don't know how many times she has told me that I needed to get a secretary, and that she would sure like to have another woman around the office." Marc laughed, remembering how Betty had even hinted at him signing on a woman partner for his office. He hadn't done that, but he had found another specialist in the same field that would add his expertise to the business.

"The new doctor that is joining me starts next month. His name is Philip Wiseman. I'm really looking forward to him being in the office. My patient workload has grown to the point that I can't give each one the attention they deserve. So I know when Dr. Wiseman gets there, he will also need a secretary. If you can't work for me, maybe you could work for Dr. Wiseman." Marc was grabbing at straws, trying his best to persuade Nancy to take the job.

Nancy knew that Marc was really trying to help her, and she knew that she needed to get a job. "Okay, how about if I come in on Monday and see how it goes?"

"Great! I'll let Betty know, and we'll get your office set up for you. It's small, and I'm sorry about that, but I think later on we could—"

Nancy interrupted, "Marc, I'm going to be your secretary. I don't need a large office. As long as I have a desk, computer, and file cabinets I think I will be fine."

Marc chuckled. "I guess you're right, but I keep thinking about how big my office is and how I like the open space of it. Besides, it's been a long time since I ever hired anyone…not since Betty…I've almost forgotten what it is like."

"But I want to get one thing straight," Nancy said, looking seriously at Marc. "While I am on the job, I will call you Dr. Carter."

"But—" Marc started to say.

"No, it's got to be that way because you need the respect in your office." Nancy was adamant.

"Betty doesn't call me Dr. Carter, and it's fine."

"But Betty has been with you forever. Everyone knows her, and she's and older woman, and it is all right. Besides, I bet she says Dr. Carter to your patients."

Marc had to agree that she did, but he still didn't like putting such formalities between him and Nancy. He wanted them to be friends…maybe they could even be close friends. He admitted that he hadn't taken much time to cultivate any close friendships since Melanie and Amber died.

"Now that that is all settled, how about if we grab a bite to eat before I take you back to your car?" Marc said. "I'm pretty hungry, and we left the cookies sitting on the table in the hallway."

Nancy laughed. "I meant to do that. They smelled so good coming over. I was tempted to eat one, so I left them on your hall table so that I wouldn't start nibbling away at them on the trip to see the house."

"Sounds like you're as hungry as I am. Let's get some really good food. Have you ever been to Lazarrio's?"

"No, I've never even heard of it. What kind of food do they serve?"

"The best Italian restaurant in Texas—you haven't dined until you've dined at Lazarrio's!"

"You sound like an advertisement! And you just took me to the best barbeque place in Texas. What's next the best hamburger place in Texas?"

"That would be Big Sam's!" Marc said jokingly "Best hamburger you ever put in your mouth. I'll take you there next."

"You're impossible!" Nancy laughed.

"Just wait—tasting is believing," Mark said as he turned the corner and headed for the Italian restaurant.

Pulling up in front of a very beautifully detailed restaurant, he circled into the driveway. Both door opened up, and a man on Nancy's side helped her out and said in an Italian accent, "Welcome to Lazarrio's!"

Nancy glanced over at Marc as he came around to her and offered her his arm. "Let's go in. You'll be glad you came with me."

Nancy lowered her voice, "This seems like an awful fancy place, Marc. I'm not dressed for someplace like this."

Marc looked her over. "You look good to me."

That made her blush. "You know what I mean. This place looks like the tuxedo and ball gown type of place."

"Wait and see. All kinds of people come here. And besides, Nancy, this is Texas. Millionaires dine in jeans in Texas!"

With a shrug of her shoulders, Nancy decided she would just enjoy it. Joe had never taken her to a place like this. In fact, if they didn't serve beer in a can, Joe never dined out anywhere.

The maître d' bowed as they came in and said, "Ah, Dr. Carter, welcome back. Would you like a window view?"

"Sure, Tony. And I'd like for you to meet a friend of mine. Nancy, this is Tony Rosetta. He is the manager of Lazarrio's."

"Hello, Tony," Nancy said.

"Ah, you have picked a beauty, Dr. Carter. I am glad to see you both tonight," Tony said as he led them to their table.

Nancy was still blushing as Tony held the back of her chair and seated her. Holding open the menu, he offered it to her with a flourish and then did the same for Marc. "Your waiter will be with you in a few moments. Could I bring you something to drink?"

"Thanks, Tony, how about some of that great coffee you have?" Marc looked at Nancy and said, "How about you, Nancy?"

"Just water please."

"As you wish, I will bring both to you in a few moments." Tony bowed again as he left.

Nancy glanced over the menu and then whispered, "There are no prices on here!"

Leaning over and whispering back, Marc answered, "That's to keep people you bring here from being too nosey! Now just relax and order what you want."

"You are incorrigible!" Nancy said as she looked over the menu again.

"Incorrigible? Maybe I should have brought my dictionary with me," he teased.

"Well, since we're in Texas, let's just say you're hopeless!" she teased back.

The waiter soon came and took their order. After he left, Marc sat back in his chair, sipping the wonderful Italian coffee that he had ordered. "Tell me about yourself, Nancy."

"There's really not much to tell, Marc. Besides, you know most of it. I have a daughter, and we moved back here after my husband died. That's all there is to know."

"I don't believe that. Tell me what kind of things you like to do?"

"Besides take care of my daughter? I don't know, maybe read?"

"You don't have any hobbies? How about before you were married? Did you do anything then?"

"I got married young actually. So I really didn't have a chance to have any hobbies. I did go fishing with my dad a lot while I was home."

"Where do your parents live?"

"They lived in Texas most of their lives, but after Joe moved us to Oklahoma, Mom and Dad moved up there to be close. Dad passed away a year ago, and Mom's been thinking about moving back so that she could be with her daughters. But I think the real reason she wants to move back is because she misses her granddaughter."

"I can understand that. Sarah is a darling girl. Anyone would miss her."

"Thanks, she can be a handful. But I wouldn't change a thing in my life if it meant giving up Sarah," Nancy said.

"I had a daughter. Her name was Amber." Marc looked down into his coffee cup, thinking.

"Yes, you mentioned her before. I'm sorry for your loss, Marc. I know it's hard to lose someone you love." Nancy remembered how she felt when her dad had passed away. She had been very close to her father, and she missed him terribly.

"It's hard to go on after you lose someone, but I know that Melanie and Amber wouldn't have wanted me to become a hermit. Which, according to Aunt Nettie, is exactly what I've become."

Nancy looked surprised. "You don't seem like a hermit to me. You're always at the hospital or at your office. Or you are over visiting with your aunt. And Sundays, you go to church. It sounds like you are a very busy man."

"Yeah, those are the exact words Aunt Nettie said. She said I was too busy. That I needed to slow down and enjoy life and not grieve forever. But how do you do that?"

"I guess you do it one day at a time," Nancy answered and then stopped. Who was she to give advice? She still wasn't over the loss of her father, nor the horrible marriage that she had been in. Maybe she should take her own advice and live one day at a time and see what happened.

The waiter came with their food, and the wonderful aroma made Nancy's stomach growl. Thankfully it wasn't very loud, and no one heard it. She put her napkin in her lap and waited for the risotto to be set in front of her. Then she waited because she knew that Marc would want to bless the food.

Marc held out his hand and said, "I usually join hands with whoever I'm dining with when I ask the blessing. Do you mind?"

Slipping her hand into his, she closed her eyes and bowed her head. She heard Marc begin the prayer, but her mind kept going back to the feel of his hand wrapped around hers. She wondered why she felt so cherished and secure. What was it about Marc that made her feel that way?

Marc tried to keep his mind on what he was saying to God, but the feel of Nancy's hand in his caused him to trip over some words and hesitate as he tried to recall what to say. What was it about holding Nancy's hand that made him want to forget everything and just pull her closer and kiss her? Quickly, he said amen, hoping that Nancy never noticed his mistakes. Reluctantly, he released her hand and let her pick up her fork and begin eating. As she lifted her fork to her lips, he couldn't help but wonder exactly what those lips would feel like under his.

Drawing his eyes away, he put a bite of his veal Marsala into his mouth without really tasting it. His eyes were drawn back to Nancy as she bit into her chicken.

"This is really good!" Nancy exclaimed

"Now you won't doubt me when I tell you it's the best Italian food in Texas."

"You do know your food…so far," Nancy continued to tease him, enjoying the easy camaraderie she felt with him, but she had to remember that this was only a short-term friendship. Starting Monday, he would be her boss, and that was something she planned on remembering!

Chapter 18

Monday morning came quickly for Nancy. She was excited and nervous at the same time. It was also Sarah's first day in a babysitter's house.

Susan had introduced Nancy to an older woman in church yesterday. Susan mention the woman had an opening in her daycare for another child. Luckily, this woman took in older children, not just babies, and the woman went to church. To top it all off, she turned out to be one of Sarah's Sunday school teachers, so Sarah was already comfortable with being around her.

Nancy closed her eyes for a moment and breathed a prayer of thanks, which seem to be coming easier for her as time passed. Things were looking so much better. She had gotten a job, even if it might be temporary, she had found a good babysitter, and Susan seemed to be enjoying their company.

A knock on her bedroom door startled her from her thoughts. "Come on in," she said.

"Hey, I was wondering if you were ready. Sarah has already had breakfast and is raring to go to Mrs. Johnson's house."

"I'm ready, I sure do appreciate you taking the time to drop Sarah off at the babysitters and drop me off at work too. Maybe I can find a cheap used car somewhere if this job works out."

"It'll all come together for you, Nancy, just give God time to work."

"I know, Susan. I was just in here telling God 'thank you' for all he's done for me so far. It really is amazing at how he has given me so much in such a short time."

"He is always good, Nancy. He's never left you. Remember that, okay?"

Nancy glanced at her watch and saw they needed to get going. "I'll do my best, but we had better head out if we are both to get to work on time."

They dropped off Sarah first and then headed over to Dr. Carter's office. Susan was driving and was talking to Nancy about her workload at the hospital.

"It's been really heavy lately. If I could, I'd get a different job, but I'm thankful for the one I have, so I shouldn't complain."

Nancy grimaced, remembering what she had promised Serena. "Oh my goodness! Susan, I am so sorry. I just remembered that I was supposed to tell you about that job at the police station."

Susan glanced over at her. "Well, you told me you didn't take it, but you never really mentioned why."

"It really doesn't matter why, but I promised Serena that I would mention the job to you. You would be perfect for the position, Susan!"

"Me? Why would it be perfect for me, but not for you?"

"Because of your skills in working in admitting in the hospital is why. The program that Serena was trying to show me was mostly Greek to me, but I thought about you and all that you do, so I mentioned your name to Serena. She told me to tell you to call her." Nancy dug around in her purse for the number. "Here is the number. Why don't you give her a call?" Nancy named the salary, plus mentioned the employee benefits.

Susan exclaimed, "Why on earth didn't you take the job? Nancy, I'm your sister, and I know you could have learned that program with ease. You were top in your graduating class, and you even were a secretary for a while before you married Joe. So what gives?"

Nancy moved uneasily. How could she explain to Susan what she felt? She knew that Susan and Tony were friends, and she didn't want to say anything bad about him.

"I...I just didn't feel comfortable there."

Susan looked at her shrewdly. "It was Tony, wasn't it? He made you feel uncomfortable."

Nancy nodded. "Yes, but I don't want to say anything bad about him. I'm sure he's probably a nice guy. It's just that…well, he reminded me of…Joe."

Susan nodded. "You don't have to explain it to me. Remember I dated Tony. I know exactly what he's like. And I will tell you we are friends, but it is because he knows I'll tell him exactly the way the 'cow ate the corn,' and he can't do a thing about it. But there is no way I'd ever marry a man like that—I'd end up in jail for murder."

Nancy laughed out loud. Susan amended her statement, "Well, probably not murder, but maybe assault and battery!"

"Tony doesn't know how well off he is for not dating you!"

"Oh yes, he does. I've told him many times." Susan laughed with Nancy. Pulling into an empty parking place to let Nancy out, she said, "I think I will call Serena, thanks for thinking of me."

Nancy smiled and got out of the car. Susan hit the window button and rolled down the passenger side window. "Hey, sis…I'll pick you up on my way home today, and then we'll get Sarah. I'll be by a little after five."

"I'll be ready! Have a great day and pray for me, I'll need it!" Nancy said as she smiled and walked into the building.

Susan waved back and was still smiling as she drove away. Out loud, she said, "Thanks, God. It's been so long since I've seen Nancy this happy. Please keep on giving her your blessings. Amen."

Nancy walked into the building. It was going to be another hot Texas day, and she was thankful she would be working inside in an air-conditioned building. Making her way toward the back, she called out, "Betty, are you here?"

"Back here, Nancy. Are you ready to start your first day?"

Nancy walked back into the small room that was to be hers. Betty was just finishing dusting the desktop.

"I just got finished dusting everything down for you. Now you have a nice clean office to start out with."

"Thanks, but that should be my job!" exclaimed Nancy. "I didn't expect you to do all of that."

"Oh, don't give it another thought, honey. I always get here much too early. And I hate just sitting around doing nothing, so I find something to do. Marc will be here in about an hour, and his first patient comes in about a half hour after that. Let's go to my desk, and I'll start showing you the procedures to check people in."

Nancy worked with Betty and was surprised at how fast she picked up on the information system the office used. Betty was showing her how to schedule appointments when Marc walked in.

"Hello, Nancy, I see that Betty's already got you working hard."

Nancy looked up, surprised that an hour had passed so swiftly. "Actually, she's done most of the work. I'm just learning."

Betty said, "Don't you believe it, Marc. Nancy picked up on the data system pretty quickly. Now I'm showing her the scheduling and appointments. She's doing fine, and I'm going to be a happy lady when I go on vacation next week."

Startled, Nancy said, "Next week? You're going on vacation next week?" She looked over at Marc.

Marc snapped his fingers. "Is it your vacation time already? I had forgotten. Maybe we ought to call a temp service for the receptionist job until you get back. I don't want Nancy to feel too stressed right at first."

Betty waved her had toward Marc and said, "Don't give it another thought. Nancy is doing so good she'll have all of this down in nothing flat."

Nancy looked skeptical, but she didn't say anything. It really didn't seem all that hard, and maybe, just maybe she could do the job while Betty was gone. At least it would give her two weeks instead of just one to find out if she really could work with Marc Carter.

Betty looked at the computer screen. "Oh, I had forgotten."

Nancy looked at her questioningly.

"You've got an appointment for Sarah tomorrow. She's supposed to see Marc at ten tomorrow morning."

Nancy said, "How could I have forgotten! Sarah has talked about it for days now. Oh dear, I might have to change that. I don't have a car yet, and there is no way I can go pick up Sarah from her babysitters and then take her back. Is there another day that I could reschedule?"

Betty shook her head. "No need for that. We've got that play area for children over there." She pointed toward a boxed off area that had books and toys and all kinds of things that could keep a child busy.

"She can't stay there for three hours. Then I would have to find a way to take her back to the babysitters after her appointment. I don't know, Betty…maybe I should just reschedule. I'll find out from Susan tonight what her days off are, then I'll…"

Marc stood in the doorway of his office and said, "I don't think that's necessary, Nancy. Just bring Sarah with you to work, and I'll take her back to the babysitters at lunch. In fact, we can all have lunch together, and you can show me where her babysitter lives."

Betty beamed, "That's a perfect solution! Good for you, Marc, for thinking of it."

"But that's unnecessary. I can just re—"

"I really would like to see Sarah, and you have an appointment. It might be a few weeks before we could work her in again," Marc broke in.

"Besides," Betty said, "I want to meet this little girl. She sounds precious, and I miss my grandchildren. Of course, I'm going to be a great-grandma in about two months. All of my grandchildren are grown or almost grown. I miss them being little where they would come and crawl up into Mamaw's lap for a hug."

Nancy said, "All right, you both win. How can I object when you gang up on me like that?"

Marc smiled. "Don't even try." He walked back into his office and closed the door.

Working with Nancy was going to be harder than he thought as he sat down in his office chair. He knew it the minute he walked into the office and saw her blond head bent over the computer. His heart gave a double beat just seeing her there. But when he had talked to her, it had gotten even harder. He wanted to tell Betty to not worry about teaching Nancy the receptionist duty right now. He had wanted her to be in his office, he had wanted to hear her talk, and he had wanted to do some teaching and training with her. He had just wanted her to be near him. Marc shook his head…what was happening to him?

Nancy tried to concentrate on what Betty was telling her, but since Marc had entered the office, she had been distracted. She had known it was Marc as soon as the door had opened. She had felt the prickling of sensation on her arms; she had felt the pure masculinity of his presence before he had said a word. It was going to be harder to work with Marc than she thought…but she could probably handle it for two weeks. It was the least she could do for all the work that Betty was doing to train her.

The day flew by with patient's coming in all during the day. Nancy and Betty went next door for a quick bite of lunch. Marc had gone over to the hospital to check on a couple of patients and was back at his desk by the time they returned.

The office closed at five but at four thirty, the phone rang. Nancy picked it up and said, "Hello, Dr. Carter's office, may I help you?"

"Yes, could I speak to Nancy Blackwell. This is her sister."

"Hey, sis, didn't you recognize my voice?" Nancy teased.

"I thought it was you, but you sounded so professional," Susan teased back.

"Oh, sure I did."

"Really, Nancy, you sounded good…but that's not why I called. Do you think you could get a ride home? I called Serena, and she told me that the only time she had free to interview me was at five. So I've got to rush just to get there."

"I…I'm sure I can find a ride."

Betty looked up and said, "I'll get you a ride."

Nancy spoke to Susan, "Betty said she would give me a ride, so don't worry about it."

"Great, I'll talk to you tonight when I get back."

"Okay, I hope it goes great for you."

"Me too. Bye."

Nancy hung up the phone and said, "Thanks for coming to my rescue, Betty. I plan on trying to find a good used car, but it will be a few months before that happens."

"Don't worry about it. I'm sure Marc won't mind giving you a ride home."

"Marc? But I thought you said you would give me a ride home!"

"You didn't hear what I said. I said I would get you a ride. I can't give you a ride because I'm going over to my grandkids' house tonight. I would have given you a ride otherwise, but Marc will be happy to do it. Just a minute, and I'll ask." Betty hopped up and went into Marc's office without knocking.

"Wait..." Nancy tried to say, but she didn't get the sentence out, and she couldn't leave because the phone rang at the same time. After rescheduling an appointment for a patient, she heard Betty behind her.

"It's all settled. Marc said he would be glad to give you a ride home. He had forgotten that you didn't have a car. So he plans on picking you up for work in the morning too."

"But he doesn't have to do that."

Marc came to the doorway with his briefcase in his hand. "I know I don't have to give you a ride. I want to give you one. Besides, you know if Sarah was here, she would be begging for a ride in my chariot."

Nancy rolled her eyes. "I know! And she will be in sheer and utter delight to see you pull up to pick her up, but I won't hear the last of it for months."

Marc laughed and said, "Your car awaits, madam."

Betty laughed, and Nancy said, "Home, James...but don't forget my daughter first!"

They walked out of the office still teasing each other. Betty waited until the door closed tightly behind them, and then she picked up the phone. Dialing a number, she waited.

"Hello?" the voice on the other end answered.

"Hello, Nettie? You'll never guess what happened!"

"What?" Nettie Matthews answered back.

"Marc and Nancy just left here together. And they were laughing and teasing each other. I think your plan is going to work."

"It's not my plan, Betty, its God's plan. He brought Nancy just at the time that Marc needed her, and she needed Marc."

Betty nodded, even though she knew that Nettie couldn't see her. "True, but you know God sometimes sends angels to help. And I've always loved being an angel!"

Chapter 19

Sarah was bouncing up and down on the bed as Nancy was getting ready to take her to work with her. Nancy couldn't get her daughter to settle down because she was so excited after riding in Dr. Angel's chariot and now getting to go to Dr. Angel's office.

"Mommy, do you think that Dr. Angel will give me a sucker if I'm a really good girl and do what he tells me to do?" Sarah asked as her blond curls bounced up and down with the rhythm of her body bouncing on the bed.

"It's Mrs. Betty that will give you a sucker, Sarah. She is a really nice lady that really wants to meet you."

"Yes, Mommy, and I would like to meet her too, but do you think that Dr. Angel will let me see inside his office? Do you think he'll let me sit on his chair? Maybe even sit in his lap? Don't you think that would be fun, Mommy?"

Nancy was only half listening. "Yes, dear, I'm sure it would."

"Mommy, do you think that Dr. Angel really likes me? I think he does. Mommy, do you think that Dr. Angel would give me another ride in his chariot?"

"Sarah, you know that Dr. Angel...I mean, Dr. Carter is coming to pick us up, so you'll get to ride in his car again."

"Goody! But do you think he likes me, Mommy? I think he does because he always calls me princess when he sees me. Mommy, am I a princess? I like pink, so I must be..."

Nancy again tuned out Sarah's questions as she was putting on her shoes. She couldn't find one of them, so she got down on her knees and looked under the bed, finding the offending shoe about midway underneath. Grunting, she scooted forward, and she heard Sarah say, "Mommy, do you think Dr. Angel will be here soon?"

"Yes, Sarah."

She could almost reach the shoe, maybe if she stretched a little bit further.

"Mommy, do you think that Dr. Angel will notice my pretty dress?"

"Yes, Sarah."

"Mommy, do you think that Dr. Angel is handsome?"

"Yes, Sarah."

Bonk! Nancy rose up too fast, startled when she realized what Sarah had just asked her, and what she had just answered. She hoped and prayed that Sarah hadn't heard her! Reaching the missing shoe, she crawled backward out from under the bed as Sarah said, "Mommy, do you think that Dr. Angel will take me to get something to eat if I'm hungry?"

Whew! Thought Nancy, *I think I dodged a bullet with the last question! Not that I don't think Marc Carter isn't handsome, he was kind and rugged, and he was definitely masculine.* Nancy sat down on the edge of the bed and finished putting on her shoes just as the doorbell rang.

Sarah jumped off the bed running down the hallway. "I'll get it. It's Dr. Angel!"

"Sarah, wait!" Nancy tried to stop her, but it was too late. Sarah had already swung the door open wide and shouted, "Mommy, it's Dr. Angel…hurry up, he's ready to go!"

"I'm coming," Nancy called out but muttered to herself, "I would have already been there if she hadn't kicked my shoe under the bed last night after being so excited about riding in his chariot!"

Glancing at herself once more as she passed the mirror, Nancy made her way to the front door. "Sorry to keep you waiting, Marc, but I had a little trouble this morning finding some things."

"It's all right. I'm early anyway, but I wanted to make sure I got here to pick you all up in time," Marc said as he opened the door for Nancy and then helped Sarah into the backseat. He had let the car seat down that was a special feature in the car when he bought it. At the time, he didn't think he would ever use it, now he was glad to have it.

When he got into the car and started to drive away, Sarah spoke up, "Dr. Angel, did you know that Mommy had to climb under her bed to get her shoe?"

"She did? Why was her shoe under there?" Marc asked with a smile, glancing in the rearview mirror at Sarah.

"Yes, she did. And I don't know why her shoe was way under the bed like that. She always kicks them off by the door."

Marc glanced at Nancy and saw that she was blushing. She looked his way and shook her head, daring him to say something.

"And you know what else, Dr. Angel?"

"What?" Marc said, expecting Sarah to say something else about the shoe.

"Mommy said she thinks you are handsome. She even hit her head under the bed when she said it."

"Sarah!" Nancy exclaimed, turning around to give her daughter a stern look. "I did not say that!"

"Yes, you did, Mommy. I asked you if you thought Dr. Angel was handsome while you were under the bed, and you said yes, and then you bonked your head."

Marc looked over at Nancy with a smile and a raised eyebrow. "So now your secret is out."

Nancy looked mortified at him and stammered, "W-what s... secret?" Could Marc have possibly figured how she felt every time she was around him?

"Well, that you think I'm handsome." He grinned.

"She does. Mommy does think you're handsome. And you know what? I think you're handsome too. But Mommy thinks you smelled good the other day too. She said so to Auntie Susan."

"Sarah, I think you've talked enough for now. It's time to zip your lip," Nancy said.

"But, Mommy, you did tell Auntie Susan that Dr. Angel smelled good and—"

"Young lady, I said that was enough," Nancy said sternly. "For your information, I said that I liked Dr. Angel's...I mean, Dr. Carter's cologne."

"Ah, another secret!" Marc teased.

Nancy turned to him and muttered, "You know too many secrets. Now let's talk about something else."

"But this was just getting interesting," Marc said.

"I'll bet it was," Nancy muttered, then under her breath, she said, "For you."

Marc was still laughing as they pulled into the parking place reserved for him. Hopping out of the car, he went around and opened up the door for Nancy and then opened up the door for Sarah and helped her get out of her car seat.

"Dr. Carter, you don't have to open up the car door for me. I'm your employee."

"You're still a lady, and as such, I will treat you like one. If it's any consolation, I also open up the car door for Aunt Nettie and any other lady that I have ride with me."

Nancy smiled and then innocently asked, "What would you do if there were four of us? It would sort of keep you busy, don't you think?"

Marc held Sarah's hand as they walked into the building, and he answered, "I haven't had that pleasure yet, but if it ever happens, I'll just tell everyone to sit until I can get to all the doors."

"See, Mommy, Dr. Angel is a gentleman, just like you..."

"Sarah, I think you have repeated enough about me today to last a lifetime. Let's just go on in, and you can play with the toys and meet Mrs. Betty."

"Rats! She was just getting to the good part," Marc said with a sly grin on his face.

Nancy just shook her head and walked through the door he held open for her. Betty was already in the office and looked up as they came in. "So this must be the princess I've been hearing about."

Sarah went over to her and said, "Yes, that's me. I'm a princess 'cause I like pink, and Dr. Angel calls me princess. But sometimes

Mommy says I don't act like a princess…" Suddenly Sarah clamped her hand over her mouth and looked at Nancy.

Through her hand, she mumbled, "Sorry, Mommy, I didn't mean to say anything else."

Nancy smiled and said, "It's all right this time, sweetie."

Betty looked curiously at all three of them and asked, "What's this all about?"

All three of them spoke at once.

Marc said, "I learned some really interesting things on the way here."

At the same time, Nancy said, "It's really nothing."

And Sarah said, "I told Dr. Angel about Mommy thinking he was handsome."

Betty's eyes lit up when she caught Sarah's words through all the talking. Instead of bringing it up, she acted as if she hadn't heard her. She said, "Sarah, would you like to go see the toys over there? I'll bet there is a book about a princess that you can look at. And if you are really good, I'll give you a sucker."

Sarah's eyes got big and said, "Mommy said you would give me a sucker, and she's right!"

"I'm sure, your mom is right about most of the stuff she said," Marc answered as he made his way into his office. Just before he shut the door, he turned and gave Nancy a wink, closing the door before she could say anything.

"Well, it seems as if you've had a very interesting morning." Betty drawled.

"Interesting for whom?" Nancy muttered.

The first part of the day passed in a mad rush with Nancy taking Sarah into the exam room at ten o'clock. Marc came in, wearing his white coat, his stethoscope around his neck.

"Dr. Angel has on his angel suit, Mommy! Does he always wear it when he works?"

"Why don't you ask him?" Nancy said.

"Dr. Angel, do you always wear your angel suit at work?" Sarah said, turning to Marc.

"Most of the time, princess, does it bother you?"

"No way! I knew you were an angel a long time ago, but nobody else did. Now everybody will know you're an angel 'cause you wear the suit," Sarah said matter-of-factly.

"Well, if I tell you a secret, would you promise to not tell anyone?" Marc whispered close to Sarah ear.

"Sure!" Sarah's eyes brightened.

"No one else really believes I'm an angel even when I wear my suit."

"Really? Boy, are they dumb!" Sarah shook her head in disgust. "Anybody could see that you're an angel just by looking. I didn't need no white suit to see it."

Marc checked Sarah over, peering into her eyes and asking her some questions. Sarah answered each one. He glanced at Nancy and asked, "Have you noticed Sarah being dizzy or bumping into things since the accident?"

"Not more than usual." Nancy said. "She's always had a slight problem since she's gotten older of being a little dizzy sometimes. It mostly happens when she's tired."

"Is she tired a lot?" questioned Marc.

"Yes, she tires easily. In fact, I'm sure she will take an N-A-P after lunch," Nancy spelled.

Sarah's bottom lip pouted. "I don't wanna take a N-A-P! I'm a big girl!"

Marc laughed. "Well, she's certainly smart for her age."

"Unfortunately for me, she remembers way too well." Nancy admonished.

"Hmmm, maybe you ought to go and see if Betty needs any help while I finish up here with Sarah." Marc grinned.

"Not a chance! I do not trust either one of you," Nancy said.

Marc finished up his exam and then said, "Nancy, I think we need a few more tests. I don't see any lingering problems from the accident. I'm going to order the MRI results brought up here, and I want to look them over again. And I would like to have a CAT scan done."

Sarah looked up and said, "A cat! I love cats!"

Marc laughed and said, "No, not a real cat. This is a big machine, and it will take pictures of your head."

"That's a silly name for a big machine that takes pictures. My mommy has a little machine that takes pictures, and she calls it a camera. Why don't they just call it a big camera?"

Nancy raised her eyebrow and looked at Marc. "Well, it's your turn."

"That's a good question, Sarah. How about if we talk about it during lunch?" Marc said.

"Can we have lunch right now?" Sarah hopped off the exam table.

"Sure, you're my last patient this morning, and I'd like to take a little longer lunch today. How about if we go by and pick up some hamburgers and take them to the park. We can eat, and then you can play for a while, and then we'll come back here to finish up the day before I take you and your mom home."

"Goody! I get to ride in your chariot again," Sarah said, hopping up and down.

"You don't have to do that, Marc. I can take Sarah to the place next door and eat," Nancy said.

Marc turned and looked Nancy right in the eyes and said sincerely, "I'm not doing it because I have to do it. I'm doing it because I want to. I'm finding out I like having two women in my life again."

Nancy didn't know what to say. She knew there was something going on between her and Marc Carter, something that seemed so real and yet so elusive. Something she wanted to grab and hold on to, yet something she was afraid to touch. Someday, she hoped that the memories of Joe and their marriage would fade. Then she would finally be free to care for a man as good as Marc Carter. Until then, she would have to be very careful because she could fall in love so easily and be hurt so much. Nancy determined in herself to keep that from happening again.

Chapter 20

Marc went through the drive through chicken place, picking up a bucket of chicken, rolls, coleslaw, drinks, and of course, a rich dessert for each one of them. Then he drove to the nearby park.

Quickly he assisted Nancy and Sarah from the car, and as Nancy started to grab the sack of food, he said, "I didn't bring you here to be a pack mule…you're my guest."

"But it's just a sack of food," Nancy protested.

"Doesn't matter. I can carry it and the blanket too."

"Blanket? Mommy, do I have to take a N-A-P?"

Marc and Nancy laughed, and Marc said, "No, princess, the blanket is to spread out on the grass so you and your mom doesn't get grass stains all over your pretty clothes."

"Oh, then you had better get the blanket because I have a new dress on that Auntie Sarah bought for me."

"And I can see that it's a dress fit for a princess," Marc said as he grabbed the blanket from the trunk of the car, and they made their way over to a place under a pecan tree.

Soon they had their feast spread out in front of them and were indulging themselves in the chicken and coleslaw. Sarah had finished off a chicken leg and then jumped up, saying, "Mommy, can I go swing and play on the playground?"

Nancy looked over at the play equipment. It was close enough where she could keep a close eye on Sarah, so she nodded her head then admonished, "If you get too hot and tired, I want you to come and rest a bit."

"No N-A-P!" Sarah said stubbornly.

"Not a nap, just a rest," her mother assured her.

"Okay!" Sarah ran to the play equipment.

Marc watched her as she climbed on the swing and started pumping her feet to get the swing moving.

"I remember teaching Amber how to start the swing," Marc said almost to himself.

Nancy reached over and, in a bold move but one that felt right, laid her hand on his where it rest on the blanket. It hurt her to see his pain and his loneliness.

"I'm so sorry about your wife and little girl. Do you want to talk about it?"

He turned and looked at her; the pain in his eyes was so real that she could feel it. Her heart started beating faster as he closed his hand over hers and said, "For the first time since they died, I really do want to talk about it. I haven't really talked about it to anyone. I haven't been able to."

Nancy waited as he continued, "No one seemed to understand. They would say they did, but they hadn't lost a wife and a child… someone they loved more than their own life. There have been so many times that I've told God…asked him, really…why didn't he just let it be me that the drunk driver had hit and killed. Why did he let it be someone so innocent as my wife and daughter?"

"Did God ever let you know why?" Nancy asked, curious as to what Marc would say.

"Not really. And I have often wondered why he never said anything to me. I would pray and pray, but most of the time I would get up each morning and just go about trying to live. At first it was so hard. All I wanted to do was stay home where I could be around the things that were Melanie's and Amber's. Then it got to where I didn't want to be home for the same reason. All of Melanie's dishes and Amber's toys were there. I couldn't bring myself to even go into Amber's room; everything was just how she left it for months. Finally, Aunt Nettie came in one day when I was working and cleared things out."

"How did that make you feel?"

His grip tightened on her hand, but she allowed her hand to stay in his. It seemed to bring him comfort, and she wanted so much to give him what little comfort she could offer.

"I was so angry with her. I didn't even want to call her. I wanted to see her and yell at her. She had no right to come and take away the things that were there. But as I drove over there, God talked to my heart. He seemed to give me a peace that I hadn't had before. By the time I had gotten over to Aunt Nettie's, I had calmed down. When I pulled into her driveway, she was sitting on the front porch, and when I got out of the car, the first thing she said was, "I was expecting you, Marc."

"Did she think you were going to yell at her?"

"I'm sure she expected it, but I didn't. She told me she wanted me to realize I was still alive, and that Melanie and Amber would always be a part of me in my heart, but that they wouldn't want me to go on living like I was. So she took away everything to shock me out of myself. I realized then that she was right. She told me she had boxed it all up, and it was in her living room. If I wanted it, I could take it back right then, but I decided not to. Instead, I told her to keep it all until later, and then I would come back for it all. Now it's been almost three years now. I told Aunt Nettie last summer to donate it all to the church's rummage sale. I wasn't going to need it anymore, and someone else might as well get some good out of the clothing and toys."

Nancy slid her hand from his and pushed back her hair, glancing over at Sarah who was still playing on the playground. She noticed that her daughter was getting quite red in the sun, but it was normal for someone with such fair complexion. Sarah was hurrying toward the merry-go-round, and Nancy let her go.

"I got rid of Joe's things a week after he died. I couldn't stand to look at them anymore either, but it was for the opposite reasons that you did it."

"I know your marriage wasn't a happy one," he said as he reached for her hand again. "I'm sorry. I can't understand how a man could ever mistreat his wife."

Nancy laughed a dry, sarcastic laugh and said, "Well, I must have done something to deserve his wrath because I saw it every day. Not at first, but it wasn't long after we were married that Joe took up drinking again, and, well…let's just say it wasn't pretty."

"No woman deserves to be treated like that, especially one as lovely as you," Marc said as his hand tightened on hers.

Nancy could feel him moving slowly toward her. She could feel the tug of his hand pulling her closer, she could see the longing in his eyes, and she was sure that hers reflected the same. She knew he was planning on kissing her, and she was going to let him. Nervously her tongue darted out and wet her lips, and she saw his eyes darken.

The touch of his lips on hers seemed to convey everything that she had ever longed for in a relationship…joy, happiness, contentment, and most of all, she felt cherished and loved.

Everything seemed to drop away, and there was only Marc and her together as his lips moved over hers in a gentle yet searching kiss that she seemed to feel clear down to her toes.

"Mommy, are you and Dr. Angel getting married? Is that why you are kissing? Kenny tried to kiss me one time, and it was yucky! I punched him."

Jerking apart, Nancy was red-faced with embarrassment. Marc turned with a smile and said, "Who is Kenny?"

"A boy that went to my preschool where my mamaw lives. He's yucky."

Marc turned toward Nancy and said with laughter in his eyes, "Was I 'yucky'?"

"It's none of your business, but I might punch you if you don't hush," Nancy retorted back.

Marc threw back his head and laughed. It felt so good to laugh, he thought.

Nancy started giggling at first and then started laughing until the tears rolled down her cheeks.

Sarah was laughing and dancing around them both. She was so excited to see her mommy laughing again. She had never seen her laugh this hard and look so happy. Daddy had always made Mommy cry and look sad, but Dr. Angel made Mommy laugh, and that was what God had promised her.

Nancy recovered first and said, "I think it's time I got back to the office. My boss might fire me."

"Nah, that old man won't do a thing to you. I've got an inside track with him," Marc said. Then he sighed. "It's been fun, Nancy. And as much as I hate to say it, I do have to get back to the office. I have a patient coming in a half hour."

Nancy got to her feet and started clearing away the food. Marc reached down and started helping clear it all away too. It amazed her that a man would do that. Joe had never offered to help her in any way at all. He had always told her that cleaning up was a woman's job; it was all she was good for. She had heard that so many times that she started to believe it.

Now as she glanced at Marc, she felt she had found someone that actually treated her like she had always longed to be treated. She thought about pinching herself to see if she was dreaming, but if she was, she didn't want to wake up.

The rest of the day crawled by with the afternoon patients. Marc hurried from one exam room to the other meeting with each patient and making each one feel special. He never hurried his patients because he felt he owed them his time, and he wanted to make sure they were all healthy. The ones that weren't, he wanted to make sure he could help them. He cared for them all, but today the patients seemed to talk longer than usual. He wanted to hurry them along so that they could close the office, and he could be with Nancy and Sarah again.

Today something had happened between them. He hadn't meant to kiss Nancy, but she was so caring, and she looked so beautiful with the sun shining down on her. She seemed to glow with care and understanding as he told her about Melanie and Amber. One thing was certain, when he was kissing Nancy, he didn't give Melanie a thought. All he could think about was how much he liked kissing Nancy and how her lips felt under his. He wasn't planning on waiting very much longer to feel them again, he thought determinedly.

Nancy worked at her desk, typing up memos and letters that Marc had placed there early in the day. The computer was a new one, and it had been easy to learn since she had worked on a similar program before she had married Joe.

Her mind wasn't on her typing, however. All she could think about was the kiss in the park. She remembered the feel of Marc's lips as they covered hers. She quit typing for a moment, reaching up and touching her lips, not even realizing she had done it at first. It was so amazing that someone would seem to care for her. She had been told so often by Joe that no one else would want her, that he had only married her because he pitied her, or that she had tricked him into marriage. She never had understood that, but she began to believe it. She soon became the shell of herself after living with Joe for a while. After Sarah was born, she came alive again, at least for a while. She had someone who loved her unconditionally and someone who needed her. It made her feel worthwhile.

Sarah had made Joe feel less wanted. He seemed to take pleasure in mocking Sarah and saying she was stupid like her mother. Nancy tried to shield Sarah from the worst of it, and thankfully she was young enough not to remember everything that happened between Joe and Nancy. Unfortunately, there were still some things that Sarah remembered more than Nancy had thought in one so young.

Sighing deeply, Nancy went back to typing. It seemed that the day would never end, and every once in a while, she looked out toward the reception area to check on Sarah. Every time she did, it seemed there was another patient waiting on Marc. Would the day never end where they could leave the office and at least she would be able to ride home with him and be near him again? Maybe she had been dreaming, maybe what she had felt was real to her but not to him. She knew that it wouldn't take much more of being around Dr. Marc Carter for her to fall in love with him. And that thought made her scared and yet excited all at the same time. What did the future hold for them? But one thing was for certain…she hoped it held another kiss!

Chapter 21

Marc was nervous as he pulled the car out of the parking lot. He couldn't remember when he had been this nervous. He thought back to the first time he had ever asked Melanie out on a date, but he had known her for a long time, and he hadn't been nervous because he knew she liked him, and he liked her. It just sort of happened for them.

He wasn't sure about Nancy. He knew she liked him enough to let him kiss her. He had felt her response, and she had definitely responded to him! But would she be willing to go out with him? A picnic in the park wasn't exactly a *date*, and neither was grabbing a bite here and there and even going out to lunch together. He wanted to take her to a nice place, one where there was a romantic atmosphere, a place where they could be alone and get to know each other.

Then Marc had a horrible thought... *What if she is mad at me for kissing her?* He cut his eyes toward Nancy, who was looking straight ahead. What if I asked her out and she said no because she didn't want me kissing her that soon? What if...what if I just have my head examined, he continued to think. *Good grief, I'm worse than a sophomore going out on his first date!*

*****

Nancy stared straight ahead; she couldn't believe that Marc had kissed her. She had thought about it all day, and now that they were together in the car, she didn't know what to say to him. She wondered what he was thinking about. Was he still thinking about the kiss, or was he disgusted with the fact that he had even kissed her? Did he regret it? Had she somehow pushed him into kissing her? Was she some kind of wanton woman? She knew she wasn't, but maybe he thought she was. Did he think she was pushing herself on him because she was desperate? Did he think she wasn't good enough for him?

Nancy couldn't remember being so nervous! She ran the palm of her left hand down her skirt to get the perspiration off and then did the same to her right hand. Goodness, it was warm in the car. She glanced down at the controls for the air-conditioning and saw they were on full blast.

She thought, *I wonder if he's mad at me. Did I do something at the office today that he didn't like? I mean other than kissing him! I need to just be bold and come out and just ask him. All he could do is fire me or tell me off or hate me…or even worse, never kiss me again.* She shook her head slightly, trying to clear it. Taking a deep breath, she turned to Marc. "Are you mad at me?" Nancy asked.

"Are you mad at me?" Marc asked.

The words came out in unison, stunning them both. Sarah perked up from the back seat and said, "Are you and Dr. Angel mad at each other, Mommy?"

Marc quirked an eyebrow and waited until Nancy answered, "No, honey, I just think we were asking each other a question. I'm waiting for his answer."

Marc scowled a little; he had been hoping she would answer first. Now the ball was back in his court.

Sarah said, "Are you mad at Mommy, Dr. Angel?"

Marc glanced at Nancy and saw the hint of laughter in her eyes; he knew then that she wasn't upset with him, so he figured he'd have a little fun first.

"Well, princess, I really don't know."

"You don't?" both Sarah and Nancy said together, although Nancy voice held some shock.

"Nope, I don't. You see, your mommy got in the car and didn't say anything to me. So I figured she must be mad at me for working her so hard today."

"She was really tired today," Sarah stated bluntly.

"Yep, she was. And I figured that the only way I could make it up to her was to take her out to dinner tonight. But you see, I figured she might be so mad at me that she would just yell, 'No way!' And there I would be, all left out again."

"I would not yell at you," Nancy said.

"Mommy wouldn't say that to you, Dr. Angel. Mommy doesn't yell," Sarah finished up.

"Well, I didn't know 'cause I don't know your mommy very well, but I would like to. The only way I can get to know her better is to take her to dinner. Do you think she would do that, princess?"

"Oh yes, 'cause I heard her tell Auntie Susan that she would—" Sarah started to blurt out.

"Sarah, you don't have to say that," Nancy said.

"Yes, she does," Marc added.

"That she would like to date you, but she only dated Daddy and didn't know how to go out on dates anymore. What's a date?" Sarah finished up.

Marc smiled and said, "I'll tell you what a date is. It's a special time between two people who want to get to know each other. A time when they can be all by themselves and have a nice dinner at a very nice place. There would be candles on the table, and they could order anything they wanted. There would be music, and maybe they might even hold hands." He glanced over at Nancy, then back to the road, but it was enough to see a slight blush on her cheeks.

"Wow, Mommy, that sounds like fun. Dr. Angel if mommy says no, I'll date you," Sarah said.

Marc laughed, and Nancy smiled. Seeing a place up ahead, he pulled the car over and turned toward Nancy. "Well, should I take you or Sarah out tonight?"

Nancy, with an impish light in her eyes, said with an exaggerated sigh, "I guess it'll have to be Sarah because I have to wash my hair."

"Okay, if that's the way..." Marc knew she was teasing and turned to Sarah.

Sarah's eyes were really big as she said, "I think I want Mommy to date you first. She doesn't really have to wash her hair. She did it last night 'cause she wanted it to smell good when she went to work 'cause—"

"Sarah, I think you've said enough." Nancy stopped her daughter before she said anymore. She had to remember to stop talking to herself when Sarah was around and to remember not to say anything she didn't want repeated…Sarah was a walking tape recorder!

Marc turned back to Nancy, a serious look in his eyes. "I really would like to take you out tonight, Nancy. Would you go out with me?"

Nancy knew that she wanted to go out with Marc more than she had ever wanted anything else. "Yes, Marc, I'll go out with you."

"Goody! I wanted to stay with Auntie Susan 'cause she lets me eat ice cream in bed when you're not home." Sarah slapped her hand over her mouth and looked miserable, then finished up, "I wasn't 'posed to tell. Now Auntie Susan won't let me." Tears came to her eyes.

Nancy had a hard time looking away from Marc, but she glanced back at her daughter and smiled. "It's okay, princess. Auntie Susan told me that she let you curl up with a bowl of ice cream while she read you a story. I'm sure she would like to do it again tonight too."

Marc got the car back on the road and drove them on over to Susan's house. Getting out of the car, he helped Sarah out and then opened the door for Nancy. As she got out of the car, he reached for her hand and said, "Is an hour long enough for you?"

Smiling, she nodded. "An hour is fine. What do I wear?"

"Just something nice, you'll enjoy it. Just to give you a hint, I'm wearing a suit and tie."

Nancy's heart beat faster, but she knew it wasn't because of where they were going. It was because Marc had moved closer to her as he held her hand. She wondered if he were going to kiss her here in broad daylight. Glancing over his shoulder toward his aunt's house, she could see Mrs. Matthews standing on her front porch, looking toward them.

"Ah, Marc, I think your aunt wants you to stop by before you leave."

Marc got the hint; Nancy was telling him they had an audience. He sighed and pulled back slightly. Dropping her hand, he said, "I'll see you later, and I'll stop by Aunt Nettie's and let her know…that's why she's standing on the porch. She wants to know what's going on."

Nancy giggled and felt like a schoolgirl. "Well, you need to tell her, and I need to hurry and get ready. I'll see you in an hour."

Marc watched her walk into the house. He got into his car and drove over to Aunt Nettie's. Something told him his aunt would be "tickled pink" to hear his news.

An hour later, Marc arrived promptly at Susan's house. After leaving Aunt Nettie's house, he had rushed home, jumped in the shower, and put on his suit. He was glad that he had to wear suits at work and had a number to choose from. He picked out his best one, fumbling with the tie but finally getting it just right.

Standing in front of the door, his hands began to sweat. In his left hand, he held a dozen red roses. He was glad he had a friend who was a florist and made quick deliveries. She had brought them to his house about fifteen minutes after he had called. She was a friend of Aunt Nettie's too. Marc sighed; he was beginning to think that Aunt Nettie and all of her friends were circling around him…but in a lot of ways, he was thankful. It was making this a lot easier on him.

Nancy answered the doorbell, and Marc's breath caught in his throat. Before him stood the most beautiful woman he had ever seen. His mind never even went to Melanie; all he could think about was the woman who stood in front of him.

Her gorgeous blond hair was done up in a gentle twist with slight curls around her ears and temples. Her dress was a beautiful sky blue with seed pearls across the shoulder. The dress swirled around the calves of her legs as she took the roses and went to find a vase to put them in.

He looked around for Sarah and Susan but didn't see them or hear them. Waiting at the door, he heard Nancy say, "Come in for a minute while I put these in water. Susan and Sarah have gone to the park."

Nancy placed the roses in the middle of the table and picked up her purse. "These are beautiful, Marc." She leaned her head down and smelled them. "Thank you. It's been years since anyone's bought me flowers."

"I'll remember that…it won't be years before you get them again," he said as she picked up her purse, and they walked out the door. Nancy made sure the door was locked then walked with Marc toward the car.

Marc drove to the edge of town and then continued driving. Nancy noticed that they were no longer in Crestmont, but she didn't know where they were.

"Where are we going?" Nancy questioned.

"I thought I would take you to the Lakeside Palace. Have you ever heard of it before?"

"No, I don't think so."

"Good, I think you'll enjoy it. It's only been built in the last year. And I've only eaten there a couple of times. I had two business dinners there, but the food was excellent, and the atmosphere was great."

"I'm sure I'll like it. So far everywhere you've taken me has been good."

"But this time is different, Nancy," Marc said in a serious tone. "This time…this time I want you to know it's a date. I'm not just taking you out for lunch or a picnic. I am taking you out on a date. I want to get to know you."

Nancy could feel her heart beat a little faster. "I like that, Marc. I would like to get to know you too."

"Then we'll have a lot to talk about," Marc said with a smile as he pulled into a parking lot. Pulling into a rounded entrance that was decorated with tiny lights all around and archway, the door opened, and a man offered Nancy his arm to help her out, "Welcome, Ms. Blackwell."

"Thank you," Nancy said, taking his hand and exiting the car.

Marc came around to her side as the man drove their car and parked it. Another man appeared and said, "The launch will be here any moment, Dr. Carter."

"That's fine. We'll set over there and watch the sunset." Marc crooked his arm and felt Nancy slip her hand through. His heart beat faster as her touch sent a tremble through him.

They walked together toward a low white marble bench. All around them was roses, and the smell was intoxicating as they stood there. Sitting down, Marc slipped her arm out of his and then took her hand. He looked over at her and said, "I like holding your hand."

"I kind of like holding yours too," Nancy said with a smile.

Just as Marc started to answer, there was a motor sound that caused them to turn and look behind them. An elegant yacht moved up close to the peer and lowered a small plank down to meet the pier.

Marc said, "Your chariot waits."

"Goodness, I've never seen anything like that, much less rode on one."

"Well, tonight you will."

Nancy felt as if she was in a dream. They walked aboard the yacht, and the captain greeted them. A steward seated them at a table that was secluded by a window. Outside the sun was going down, and the lights all around the lake was twinkling on. Nancy marveled at the beauty, but more than anything else, she marveled at the thought of someone caring enough about her to bring her here.

Marc couldn't take his eyes off his date. He knew in his heart that this was the woman he wanted to spend the rest of his life with. His mind went to Melanie, only briefly. Then he put her back into that special corner of his heart, knowing that this is what she would have wanted for him.

He reached over and took Nancy's hand again across the intimate table and said, "Do you like it?"

"Oh, Marc! I've never seen anything so beautiful!" she breathed. "Thank you for bringing me here."

"It's my pleasure. And I don't think I've ever seen anything so beautiful either," Marc said, his eyes never leaving Nancy's face.

She blushed as she read his thoughts. It was hard for her to accept what he said because Joe had never told her she was pretty, much less beautiful. She put Joe from her mind, pushing him away with a force and a promise to quit letting him rule her life from the grave, just like Susan had told her he was doing.

Marc said, "Tell me about you. I want to know all about Nancy Blackwell."

"What do you want to know?"

"I want to know what your favorite color is. What's your favorite flower? What do you like to do? All of that kind of stuff."

"That's a tall order, Dr. Carter."

"That's just the beginning."

"But I don't want to spend all night talking about me, I want to know about you too," Nancy said.

"We'll try to get to that too," Marc assured her.

Nancy raised an eyebrow. "Ah…how long do you plan on staying on this boat?"

Marc laughed. "Well, I guess we'll have to save some stuff for the next time."

Nancy smiled. What a nice thought… Marc had said there would be a next time. He wanted to date her again. She was surprised that she really wanted to be with Marc, wanted to get to know him. It seemed as if her whole outlook on life, and love, had changed. Maybe love wasn't as painful as she had thought. Maybe, just maybe, it might be possible to love someone and have them love you back. Tonight, Nancy thought, anything was possible.

Chapter 22

Nancy glanced at the calendar that was attached to the wall by the receptionist desk; she was amazed that the summer had passed so quickly. The cooler September air was a wonderful relief from the summer heat wave that had swept through the first part of August.

Now Sarah was in kindergarten every day, and when she got out, she was picked up by a woman from church who babysat for Nancy until she got off work. Nancy smiled thinking of all the good things that had happened in her life since she had moved to Crestmont and started going back to church.

It seemed like everything was finally working out in her life. Sarah had settled into kindergarten like a duck to water. She loved having the kids to play with all day long, and she was already learning her alphabet!

Nancy had a good job working in Marc's office. When she thought about her job, her mind automatically went to Marc. What a blessing he had been in her life! He had given her a job, helped her pick out a car, and picked her up every Sunday morning for church.

Nancy felt renewed in her faith toward God. Before she moved to Crestmont, she had felt as if God had forgotten her. She had somehow slipped through the cracks of the church where she had been attending in Oklahoma. No one had come to check on her after she had quit going, and that had really hurt her. Then Joe's drinking had gotten worse...so Nancy just figured God was too busy with other people to really care about her anymore. After Joe's death, moving back to Texas and going back to church, Nancy felt that God hadn't forgotten her—he still cared.

She heard the door to Marc's office open up, and his footsteps stopped behind her chair. Marc said, "Was that the last patient of the day?"

Turning, she smiled. "Yep, that was the last one. And since tomorrow is Saturday, you don't have any more patients to worry about until Monday morning. Dr. Wiseman is on call this weekend, and that leaves you free."

"Good, because I have something I want to do, but I want you to go with me."

"Oh? Where are you planning on going?"

"Let's just say it's a surprise." Marc smiled as he glanced at his watch. "Why don't we close up for the evening? It's five minutes to closing. I don't think five minutes is going to hurt, and I'm sure the boss won't say anything."

Nancy grinned. "Well, if you're sure I won't get into trouble."

"Positive, let me go get my jacket, and we'll head on out."

In just a few minutes, they were both seated in Marc's car and headed out of town. Nancy vaguely remembered some of the places they passed, but she still didn't know where they were going.

It became clear when Marc turned the car into a winding tree-lined driveway. They were going to the Victorian house they had looked at months before! Nancy felt the excitement well up inside. She had loved the Victorian home and had dreamed about it for weeks, but she was sure that the home had sold by now, so maybe Marc knew the new owners, and he was taking her to meet them.

"This is the Victorian home that we looked at," Nancy said

"Yep, sure is. I thought you'd like to see it again."

"I fell in love with that house! Do you know the new owners?"

"I do, and I'm sure they will be pleased that we've decided to drop in."

Nancy looked at Marc. "Do they know we're coming?"

"Yep, the owners know. Now just sit back and enjoy the view when we round this last curve."

Nancy did just as he asked. This was the best part of the whole driveway. It rounded a curve and came up over a slight rise. Then there in front of them was the gorgeous Victorian home that she had loved.

Glancing at the house, she said, "That's sort of funny."

"What is?"

"Well, if this would have been my home, I would have put up curtain in the windows first thing. The new owners must just be getting settled or something. How long ago did they buy the house?"

"Only about a month ago, so they're fairly new at the redecorating stuff. They don't really know much about it at all. That's one of the reasons I brought you over. I thought you could give them some pointers."

Nancy shook her head. "I can't do that! I'm sure my taste and theirs is totally opposite! What if I were to tell them something they didn't like? I'm more of a traditional person when it comes to decorating, and they might be modern."

"Nope, I think they would be very interested in what you have to say," Marc said as he pulled up in front of the house. Getting out of the car, he walked around and opened her door. He held her hand in his as they walked up the steps. He stopped at the door and then reached into his pocket and pulled out a set of keys.

Nancy looked at him in puzzlement. Why was he getting his keys out? Did the owners give him a key? Maybe they were really good friends and—

"Come on in," Marc said as he swung the door open.

Nancy walked inside. The house was still totally empty, and their footsteps echoed in the hallway. Glancing around, she thought she would see the new owners coming to greet them, but the house seemed to be empty.

"Well, what do you think?" Marc asked.

"What do you mean?" Nancy asked in bewilderment.

"I want to know how you think the house should be decorated."

"Marc, I'm confused. There's something else going on here, and I don't know what. But why don't you tell me why I'm supposed to tell you how I would decorate the house."

Marc held up his hand. "Wait, just wait. I'm getting a little ahead of myself here. Come on, I want to take you to the backyard."

Their footsteps echoed through the house as they made their way through the side door that led to the back. As they rounded the corner, Nancy could see a table sitting in the middle of the lush green lawn. The lawn had been newly mowed, and the table was decorated with a white tablecloth and two place settings and covered dishes.

"Come on, it's dinnertime," Marc said as he tugged on her hand.

"Marc, what is all of this?"

"I wanted you to be my first dinner guest in my new home. And the evening is still warm enough so that we can eat outside. I had it planned both ways, just in case."

"You…you bought this house?" Nancy stammered.

"Yep, I fell in love with it as much as you did when we saw it, but I didn't buy it right away because I wanted to pray about it. I figured if it was God's will for me to have it, then it would still be on the market when I was ready."

"Marc, that's wonderful! I'm so happy for you."

Marc got up from his chair and came to Nancy's side. Getting down on one knee, he reached out and held her hand. Nancy knew what was coming; the knowledge excited her and yet calmed her. She knew she loved this man who was kneeling in front of her. She was ready to share her life with him if he asked.

"Nancy," Marc began, then stopped, and started again. "Nancy, I didn't think I would ever be doing this again, but I've fallen in love with you and with Sarah. I want to share my life, this house, and my love with you both. Would you…would you marry me, Nancy?"

Nancy's eyes filled with tears. Marc was nervous. For the first time since she had known him, he seemed unsure of himself. She reached out with her other hand and touched his cheek. "Marc, I love you too. I didn't think I would ever want to marry again, but I do…I want to marry you too."

Marc's eyes lit up at her words, and he leaned forward, cupping her neck with one hand, and drew her down to him. Their lips met, first with a gentle, sweet kiss, and then feeling the love toward each other exploding like fireworks on a July 4 night. They drew closer together seeming to seek in each other the love they had just spoken of.

Marc drew back first but only slightly. Nancy felt his sigh on her lips and then a sweet kiss again. He then rested his forehead on hers as he said, "You had me worried there for a few minutes…you started to cry."

Nancy smiled. "It was tears of joy, not sorrow."

Marc nodded, then stood up, drawing her to him. He slipped his arms around her waist and exulted in the way her arms slid around his neck as if wanting to hold on to him forever.

"I have something for you, Nancy," Marc said as he pulled away slightly to reach into his pocket. "I was supposed to give you this as I asked you to marry me, but I got it sort of backward."

In his hand, he held out a box. She let go of his neck and stoked the velvety smoothness, then lifted the lid. Inside was a beautiful diamond surround by sapphires. It was the most beautiful ring she had ever seen.

"Marc! It's gorgeous!"

"The sapphires remind me of your eyes, and the diamond shows how much I love you. It's not real big, but if you want to choose a different one, we can pick it out together."

"No! I love this one. I have never liked really big, flashy jewelry. This one is perfect." Nancy held out her hand and said, "Mr. Carter, would you be so kind as to put the ring on my finger?"

Marc blushed; he had forgotten that part too! Holding her hand, he took the ring from the case and slipped it on the third finger of her left hand. Looking into her eyes, he said, "Nancy, you've made me the happiest man on earth tonight. I love you so very, very much."

"And I love you, Marc Carter. I love you with all my heart."

Marc glanced over at the table, their food still untouched. "I guess we had better eat. The food is getting cold."

Nancy smiled. "It smelled good when we sat down, and I don't mind cold food."

After they finished their meal, they walked through the house hand in hand. Marc was enjoying watching Nancy get excited about the possibilities of decorating each room with different things. His heart was full as he listened to all of the plans she started making for their house.

Soon it was time to leave, and as they walked to the car, Nancy looked back at the house once more with a prayer of thanksgiving in her heart, "Lord, you haven't forgotten me after all. You have blessed me beyond measure with a wonderful life, and I want to live it for you."

Chapter 23

Nancy and Marc planned a November wedding. Nancy wanted it to be around Thanksgiving because she was so thankful to the Lord for all of the blessings he had given to her.

Marc teased her and said, "Thanksgiving? That is a long way off. Can't we get married a little sooner?"

"How much sooner?" Nancy queried.

"How about next week?"

Laughing, she answered, "There is no way I could get everything ready by next week. Besides Thanksgiving is only two months away, and the time will go fast."

Marc replied, "I doubt it. It will seem to crawl by, I just know it."

Every evening, they were together, either at Susan's house, Aunt Nettie's, their new home with Sarah as chaperone or at church. Word quickly spread about Marc and Nancy's engagement, and everyone at church congratulated them. Well, almost everyone. Mary had been a regular for quite a few months now, but Nancy noticed that when the announcement was made about her and Marc, Mary got up quickly and left. She didn't return that day either. Nancy had known that Mary cared for Marc, and she felt sorry for her. Someday, she would try to get to know Mary. Maybe they could at least be friends.

But that didn't dim the joy that seemed to surround Nancy. It was with her everywhere she went. She just seemed to bask in the love she felt, not just from Marc but from God.

Finally, her life was smoothing out. The rough places were being replaced, the heartaches were being forgotten, and the hurts were being healed. Nancy knew it was all because of God, and she was so thankful that she had let Susan talk her into going back to church.

She had called her mom and told her about Marc. Her mother was thrilled and was coming next week to see all of them and to meet the man her daughter had fallen in love with. At first she sounded worried, but after Susan talked to her and told her what a good man Marc was, she was excited and happy for Nancy. Nancy knew that her mom was just scared that she would make another mistake, just like she had with Joe.

Nancy was putting on her shoes when Sarah came barreling into the room. "Mom, I'm ready for Sunday school! Are you ready? Did you know the teacher is supposed to take us out to the playground today for Sunday school? She said that God made everything, and we get to get stuff off the playground that God made. I think I'm going to get the swing set."

Nancy spoke up, "Sarah, God didn't make the swing set."

"Then who did? It's at the church…so God had to make it."

"No, princess, God made the trees and the grass and the flowers—"

"All the flowers are gone now, Mommy. Why didn't God let the flowers stay all the time?"

"Well, because there are different times of the year. You know that we just got finished with summer, and now its fall."

"Yep, 'cause all the leaves fall off the trees. That's why it's fall."

Nancy laughed. "Well, that's as good a reason as any I've heard, but the real name for this season is autumn."

"Ahhtumm, that's a funny name."

"Do you know what comes after autumn?"

"My schoolteacher said winter comes next. It's when things die and go to sleep. Why do things die, Mommy? Why didn't God make it where nothing died?"

"Nothing lives forever, sweetie, nothing but us. We are the only thing God made that will live forever someday."

"That's when we go to heaven, huh?"

"Yes, it is. But right now it's time to go to Sunday school."

"Yippee! And Dr. Angel will be here to pick us up…"

"Not today, sweetie. Marc had to go to the hospital to check on a patient. We're going to be riding with Auntie Susan today, and that way Marc will be able to bring us home in his car."

"Goodie!" Sarah skipped out of the room and then stopped and glanced back at Nancy as she said, "Mommy, I'll be glad with Dr. Angel can be my daddy, won't you, Mommy?"

Not waiting for an answer, Sarah skipped on into the living room, but Nancy answered her anyway, "Yes, darling, I'll be really glad when he's your daddy because that will make him my husband!" Just thinking about being a wife to Marc brought color to her cheeks and butterflies to her stomach.

Marc was certainly right when he said that the time would creep by until Thanksgiving! It was taking forever. Sighing, Nancy followed Susan and Sarah out to the car, and they made their way to church.

The service that morning was uplifting, and Nancy thoroughly enjoyed it. She enjoyed it even more when Marc slipped into the pew beside her. He had taken longer than he figured at the hospital, and that had made him a little late to church. But he was there beside her, and she felt his hand as he reached out and encircled hers.

She glanced up at him and smiled. As she turned back to face the front of the church, there was a scurrying of feet. Everyone turned as one of the Sunday school assistant's hurried toward where Nancy and Marc were sitting.

"Mrs. Blackwell, something is wrong with Sarah!"

The words rang in the church as Nancy leaped to her feet, "What?"

Marc was right beside her, then he ran past her as he made his way outside. He had seen the children around the playground when he had pulled up. Sarah had waved at him as he hurried inside. Now as he rushed out the door of the church, he could see her little body crumpled beside the swing set.

Running as fast as he could, he reached in his pocket and dialed 911. They needed an ambulance immediately.

The teacher was kneeling beside Sarah's prone body as Marc, and then Nancy arrived. The teacher was crying. "I don't know what happened, Dr. Carter! She was laughing and playing, and then she just collapsed."

"Did she fall off the swing?" Marc asked as he started to check Sarah's vital signs.

"No, she had just come over to the swing, and she hadn't gotten on to it yet," the distraught teacher said.

"Marc, what's wrong with her? Is she going to be alright?" Nancy was kneeling beside her daughter. She reached out to pull her into her lap when Marc stopped her.

"Don't move her yet. Let's wait until the ambulance gets here. I've already called for them, and they should be here any minute."

"Please, God, let them hurry!" Nancy prayed.

Susan, who had been substituting for a Sunday school teacher today, came rushing up beside them. It wasn't long until the entire congregation was gathered around, and you could hear prayers going up for Sarah.

The wailing of the ambulance seemed familiar to Nancy. It was just like the day that Sarah had gotten hit by the car. Marc had been there that day too. Only now, behind her, were the people of God. And they were praying, asking God to help Sarah and to heal her.

They soon had Sarah loaded into the ambulance with Marc and Nancy beside her. Susan said she would meet them at the hospital. Nancy watched as Marc and the paramedics worked over her daughter.

"Why, God? What has Sarah done to deserve this? Our lives were getting better, and now there's something wrong with my precious, sweet daughter. Why?"

Nancy found herself questioning God all over again. It was as if time had gone backward, and she was back with Joe wondering why their lives were so messed up and why God didn't do something about it.

But this time, it wasn't something Joe had done to her. This was Sarah…surely God would realize that Sarah hadn't done anything wrong. She was just a child…barely out of being a baby. Why would God let something happen to someone as young as Sarah?

Questions without any answers rolled around in her head. She tried to pray, but nothing would come out except why. She wanted to believe that God had a purpose in all of this, but what good could come of this?

They rushed Sarah to the emergency room while Nancy went to the front and filled out the paperwork. One thing she was thankful for was that she now had insurance because she worked for Marc. She finally finished up with the paperwork, then asked, "Can I see my daughter now?"

"Come on back, Mrs. Blackwell. Dr. Carter is still there with her."

She walked into the room and heard Marc say, "I want these tests done STAT."

The nurse nodded, and they soon had Sarah on her way to do more tests. Nancy waited until Sarah disappeared in the elevator, and then turned to Marc, "What tests are you having done? What's wrong with her? Is it because of the car that hit her?"

Marc rubbed his hand through his hair in frustration. "I don't know what's wrong yet. I've sent her up for an MRI. There's something we're missing, but I just don't know what."

Nancy could tell he was frustrated and watched as he walked over and picked up Sarah's chart again, reading it through while they waited for her to come back.

"Nancy, I'm putting Sarah in ICU."

"But you don't know what's wrong with her, maybe she just got sick…maybe she just played too much and got overheated."

Marc turned and put his hands on Nancy's upper arms. "Nancy, she wasn't sweating when we got to her. Her face wasn't even flushed. You heard the teacher say she hadn't even gotten on the swing. I want to put her in ICU so that she can have around the clock care for the next twenty-four hours. The tests will be back in about an hour. We'll have to wait and see what they say."

It seemed an eternity to Nancy before Sarah was wheeled back down to the emergency room. Marc called up to the MRI and was told they would have the test results to him in a few minutes.

Nancy saw Susan in the waiting room and went out and told her what she knew, which wasn't much.

"We're praying, Nancy. Sarah will be okay. I'm going to be leaving here in just a little while. Mom's catching an emergency flight from Oklahoma City in about an hour. She'll be here in a little less than two hours. I'm going to have to leave soon so that I can pick her up. It takes about an hour to drive to the airport. But I'll bring Mom here as soon as she comes in. I know she'll want me to."

"But...but why is Mom coming? I thought she was going to be coming in November?"

"She just felt like she should come now. I called her to pray for Sarah, and she told me she was getting a flight to come. I didn't argue with her, Nancy. Sarah is her only grandchild."

Nancy nodded and then turned when she heard her name called. It was the nurse. "Mrs. Blackwell, Dr. Carter wants to see you immediately."

Nancy knew something was wrong. She felt it down deep in her heart; she knew that the news that Marc had for her wasn't good.

Marc, his face bleak, waited for her beside Sarah's bedside. "Nancy, I got the test results back."

"What's wrong?"

"Has Sarah ever had a severe blow to the head other than the car hitting her?"

"W...why do you ask?"

"Nancy, it's important! The MRI has picked up a bone fragment. It is in her brain, and it could kill her. From the time that it happened until now, it has moved. If it moves anymore..."

"No! No! Dear God, no!" Nancy wailed. "I... I tried to get Joe to take her in... I knew. I knew something was wrong, but he wouldn't let me. He said that it would be okay...and it was, until now. Oh, God, I've killed my own daughter!" Nancy said as blackness engulfed her.

Chapter 24

Nancy came to with Marc bent over her calling her name. "Nancy! Come on, I've got to get Sarah to surgery, come on!"

She was lying on the floor with three nurses standing over her, one with a vial of some foul smelling stuff holding it under her nose. She coughed and sat up; her mind confused for a moment.

"What...what happened?" she asked as she held on to Marc's arm

"You passed out, but we don't have much time, honey. You've got to give me permission to operate on Sarah! I've already called two other surgeons in. They are in the surgery room getting ready. We need your signature to start," Marc insisted urgently.

"But...Joe... I," Nancy stammered.

"Honey, Joe's gone. It's Sarah you have to worry about."

Nancy turned as a nurse laid her hand on her shoulder. "Ms. Blackwell, Sarah has come to and is asking for you."

Nancy jumped up from sitting on the floor and rushed toward Sarah's bed. "Sarah, princess, Mommy's here."

"Mommy?" Sarah's weak voice whispered.

"I'm here, baby girl."

"Is...Dr. Angel here?" Sarah asked.

Marc stood on the other side of the bed and reached out and held Sarah's hand.

"I'm here, Sarah."

"I...I talked to God, Mommy. He...told me..." Sarah closed her eyes for a minute.

"Don't talk, sweetie. Marc is going to take you up to another room, and you'll be all better when he gets done." Nancy hoped what she was saying was true, but she knew there were no promises.

Sarah opened her eyes and looked at her mom. "It…will be okay, Mommy. God loves me."

Tears falling down her cheeks, Nancy groaned and looked up at Marc. "Tell me what you are going to have to do."

Glancing down at Sarah, he said, "I'll be back in a minute, princess. You just rest. I'm going to talk to your mommy."

Sarah answered by closing her eyes. Marc motioned for Nancy to step from the room, and he took her over to the desk where the MRI results were laying.

"There is a bone fragment. You can see it right here." Marc pointed to the MRI scan. "You can see here where it came from, but it is an old injury. I don't know what happened to cause it. All I know is that the bone fragment has now moved, and if it goes much further, we can't reach it. It could cause Sarah serious damage, or…" his voice trailed off.

"Or she could die, right?" Nancy asked.

With a deep sigh, he said, "Yes, she could die. I'm not going to keep anything from you, honey, but this is a serious operation. I can't promise you that it will all go well, but I can promise you that I will do the best I can, and we have two more of the best neurosurgeons in this area who will be working right beside me. On top of all that, we have God."

Nancy closed her eyes; she didn't want her baby going away from her. This was out of her hands, and she felt completely helpless. She knew that there was no other way; if there had been, Marc would have told her.

"Give me the papers, I'll sign them," she spoke softly. As Marc started to turn away, she grabbed his arm and held on. "Marc, would you…could you make sure that you are the one that will come and tell me…I don't want to hear it from someone else."

He pulled her into his arms, tucking her head next to his shoulder. He could feel her trembling as he held her. "Honey, I'll be out as soon as the operation is over, I promise."

She raised tear filled eyes to his and nodded. He let go and hurried to the nurse's station, telling them to get the paperwork prepared and to get Sarah up to the operating room immediately.

A nurse came and put her arm around Nancy, leading her over to a chair in front of the desk so that she could sign the papers. An orderly hurried into the trauma room and began to wheel Sarah's bed down to the elevator. Nancy hurried to her daughter's side one last time. Bending down, she kissed her gently on the cheek and said, "Mommy loves you, Sarah. When you wake up, I'll be there."

Sarah smiled slightly and said, "I love you too, Mommy. Don't cry, God will be with me...and Dr. Angel will be there too."

"I know, sweetie, I know." Nancy had to stand back as the elevator doors opened, and the orderly pushed the bed in. As the doors closed, Nancy stood there wanting one last glimpse of Sarah.

The nurse came to her again and gently led her back to the paperwork. Nancy signed everything where she was told to but didn't hear a word that was being said. All she could think about was Sarah.

The nurse was asking her something, and Nancy realized she hadn't answered, "I...I'm sorry, what did you say?"

"We have a waiting room in surgery, but Dr. Carter said it would be about a two-hour surgery. If you would like to wait there, you are welcome to. We also have a chapel just a few doors down from the waiting room. If you will let the receptionist know where you are, they will let the doctor know where to find you."

Nancy understood and then said, "My...my mother and sister will be coming here to see Sarah. Can they find me there?"

"I'll be here the rest of the evening, so I will make sure to get them to you. What is your sister's name?"

"Susan Montgomery."

"Oh, I know Susan! She worked here until a few months ago." The nurse supplied. "Sure, I'll let her know where you are. Don't worry, Ms. Blackwell, your daughter is in good hands, and the Lord knows all about it."

Nancy tried to smile, but all she could manage was a slight quivering of her lips. "Thanks."

"Here, let me call a volunteer to show you the way to the waiting room and the chapel." The nurse put in a call, and soon an elderly lady with gray hair was standing beside them.

"Grace, this is Ms. Blackwell. Her daughter was just taken to surgery. Could you show her where the waiting room and the chapel is?" the nurse said as she introduced the volunteer to Nancy.

"I sure will. Come along, Ms. Blackwell, I'll make sure you are comfortable and will do all I can for you."

Nancy followed the volunteer as if she were in a trance. All around her was the hustle and bustle of a busy hospital, but she didn't notice anything. All she could think of was her precious little girl lying on a bed, having major surgery done.

There had never been a time in Sarah's short life that Nancy hadn't been there. She was there for everything from a scratch to the time that Joe…

Bile rose up in Nancy's throat as she thought of Joe. It was his fault that Sarah was having surgery now, and it was his fault that this was even happening. If he would have let her take Sarah to the doctor when—she stopped thinking as they got to the waiting room.

"Would you like some coffee, dear?" Grace asked.

"N…no thank you, I'll be fine."

"If you need anything at all, just let the receptionist know. We are here to help in any way we can."

Nancy nodded and sat down in a blue vinyl chair. She was the only person in the waiting room, and she looked around restlessly. She needed something to take her mind off Joe and what was happening to Sarah.

Looking over at a side table, she noticed a hard bound Bible. Reaching out, she picked it up and held it in her hands. Slowly she opened the book and let her mind settle on the scripture in front of her. Her trembling finger traced the words in Psalms, "The Lord watches over all who love him…"

Closing her eyes, she prayed, "God, I know that Sarah loves you. I've tried to love you too. But I haven't done a good job. Please be with my baby girl, not for me God but for Sarah. She has so much to live for. She can do so much good in this world…please…

please..." She couldn't finish her prayer; she didn't really know what to say, only that she wanted God to do a miracle for her daughter.

She took the Bible and held it close to her heart, drawing strength from its very presence. Laying her head back against the wall, she closed her eyes and fell asleep.

*****

Marc hurried from Nancy's side and rushed into the operating room to prep for surgery. He knew that it was a rush against time for the little girl he had come to love. He was determined to do all that he could to make sure that Sarah lived a long and healthy life, but he also knew it was all in God's hands. Just as Melanie and Amber was in God's hands.

Finishing up, he walked into the surgery room just as Sarah was wheeled in. She was looking at him, and he could see a slight smile on her face.

Walking over, he laid his hand on her head, pushing back her blond curls. "How're you doing, princess?"

"Okay. But Mommy's not doing good." Sarah frowned a little.

"Your mommy loves you. She just wants you to get better. And that's why you're here. We're going to try to make you all better." Marc was trying to divert Sarah's attention away from everything that was going on around her so that she wouldn't be scared of all the machines and activity.

"But Mommy was crying. Dr. Angel...I talked to God. Will you give me a 'cross your heart' promise?" she said as she reached up and took his hand.

He felt her small hand hold on to his as he said, "I'll do my best, princess. What do you want?"

"I want you to cross your heart promise that if I go to heaven, that you will take care of Mommy. You see, she'll be really sad, and I won't be able to give her any more kisses. Will you do that for me, Dr. Angel?"

Marc swallowed a lump the size of a baseball in his throat as his hand closed tightly over Sarah's. "I cross my heart. I will take care of your mommy, honey."

From across the room, Marc hearted the sound of sniffles, looking up he saw Mary wipe away a tear from her eyes, and he knew that she had overheard their conversation and realized she would be one of the nurses helping them with the operation. "I cross my heart promise you, Sarah."

With a slight smile, Sarah closed her eyes and said, "Goody." It was the last word she spoke because the anesthesia started working.

Nancy didn't realize she had fallen asleep until a hand touched her shoulder. "Nancy, Mom's here."

Jerking her head up, she felt a kink in her neck and then realized where she was. "What time is it?" she asked frantically.

"It's six o'clock. Have you heard anything about Sarah yet?"

"No, and I was supposed to hear by five thirty at that latest!" She rushed over to the receptionist.

"Have you heard anything about Sarah Blackwell?" Nancy asked the elderly volunteer receptionist. Grace must have gone off duty, for this was a different woman.

Checking her list, the woman said, "No dear, nothing yet, but I will let you know as soon as we do."

Nancy turned toward her mom and Sarah, tears filling her eyes. "I don't know why it's taking so long. Marc said it would be two-hour surgery."

Her mom came and put her arms around her daughter, drawing her close. "Now, honey, sometimes that happens in surgery. The doctors don't always know when they go in exactly how long it will take. I'm sure Sarah is just fine. We prayed all the way here, and I feel like God is guiding the doctor's hands."

Nancy looked at her mom and sister with a bleak expression. God had let her down too many times to feel like he was in control this time. No, it was all in Marc's hands, not God's. But somehow, this didn't give her the comfort that she thought it would.

Sitting down in one of the vinyl chairs again, her mom sat beside her, and Susan sat in the row facing her.

"Tell us what happened, honey," her mom said.

"I...I don't really know...at least I'm not sure. We found Sarah collapsed on the playground, and the MRI showed a floating bone fragment. Marc said he had to remove it immediately because it posed a danger for Sarah."

"A bone fragment!" exclaimed Susan. "Did it happen when the car hit her?"

"Marc doesn't think so," Nancy said but didn't elaborate any further. She couldn't because if Sarah didn't make it, it would be all her fault.

"Have you eaten anything?" Susan asked.

Nancy glanced at her watch and said, "I ate some cereal before church this morning."

"Nancy!" her mom exclaimed. "You've got to eat to keep your strength up for Sarah. She's going to need her mommy more than ever after the surgery."

"I know, Mom, but I just don't feel like eating. Besides, I'm not leaving here because Sarah could be out of surgery any minute, and I want to know what has happened."

Susan nodded, then said, "We understand that, but I'm going down to the cafeteria. They usually stay open until seven o'clock. I'll grab us all a bite to eat. Mom and I didn't stop anywhere either, and I know Mom is probably hungry. I'll be right back."

Nancy leaned back against the cold vinyl and watched as her mom brought out a small Bible. "Nancy, let's pray. I just feel like we should ask God to put his protection around our baby girl."

"You pray, Mom, I'm just too tired."

"All right. Dear Heavenly Father, we know that you are watching over our Sarah. She is in your hands. And you know that we love her very much. Father, we want to ask you to be in that operating room with Sarah. Stay right beside her bed and whisper in her ear how much we love her. Guide the surgeon's hand as he does what he has to do. In Jesus's name, we pray. Amen."

Nancy looked at her mother after the prayer and then said in a choked voice, "Do you really believe that God heard your prayer, Mom?"

"Why, of course, he did!" her mom said with confidence. "Don't you?"

"My faith isn't very strong right now, Mom. It just seems like I was feeling as if God really cared again when this happened. Now I don't know what to think."

"Honey, you've got it all wrong. God loves us no matter what. Just because things don't go our way doesn't mean that God doesn't care about us. He loves you, and he cares about your life." Mrs. Montgomery reached out and pulled Nancy close to her like she had when she was younger.

"Honey, do you remember when Dad died?"

She felt Nancy nod as her tears soaked through her blouse. "I questioned why God didn't step in and heal your dad. He was a good man, and I felt like I needed him, but I didn't ever question whether or not God loved me and cared for me. I realize now more than ever that God has cared for me and taken care of me. The Bible says that we are all headed to the grave, and it was God's timing for your dad. It wasn't my timing, but it was God's, and he knows what is best for us."

Nancy raised a tear stained face and, in a shaky voice, said, "Do…do you think God wants to take Sarah? I don't think I could stand that, Mom. I really don't."

Her mom patted her back. "Now, now, don't think that way. Let's just believe that God has brought you here at this place for a miracle to happen. Nancy, honey…think about it. In Oklahoma, we live in a really small town, and there is no big hospital close by. If this would have happened in Oklahoma, Sarah might not be alive at all. She could have died before we could have gotten her to a hospital that could have taken care of her."

Nancy nodded again, feeling a little better. Her mom was right; it would have been nearly an impossibility to have gotten Sarah immediate care if this would have happened in Oklahoma. And what were the chances of having a top neurosurgeon at the church…and one that already loved her and Sarah?

Susan came back carrying a tray with three sandwiches and some coffee. Nancy gratefully took the coffee and sipped it, but she still couldn't eat anything. Susan gave a sandwich to their mom and sat down with the other one. None of them ate much, but Mrs. Montgomery did coax Nancy into taking a few bites.

Time continued to pass slowly; the minute hand of the clock on the wall continued to tick, but still the three women sitting in the waiting room didn't hear anything.

Finally, Nancy couldn't take it anymore. She got up and said, "Mom, I'm going to the chapel for a while. If they call, please come and get me."

Smiling, her mother said, "Of course, dear."

Nancy walked into the dimly lit chapel and went to the front. It was a small sanctuary with only three benches, but she felt the need to be close to the front. Sitting down on the padded seat, she started praying, really praying for the first time since Sarah had collapsed.

"Father, I'm such a selfish person. I don't know why I'm like I am, but I don't want to be this way. My sweet precious daughter is having surgery, and I couldn't think about anything except how I would feel if you took her to be with you. I don't want you to do that, Father, but if you know that Sarah would be better off in heaven than with me, then... I... I release her to you."

Nancy started crying, deep sobbing cries as she felt a sudden peace come over her. She looked around because she felt someone... or a presence in the room with her. As she looked, she saw no one. Burying her face in her hands, she continued to weep and pray. Giving God everything that she had held back from him, she gave him her life and her will. And this time it was real, and not just for what God would do for her.

Suddenly a hand was laid gently on her shoulder. Raising her face from her hands, she saw Marc as he sat down beside her. He didn't say anything for a moment, and she braced herself for the news of her daughter's death.

Marc looked at his hands, which were still trembling from the tedious surgery. He was still amazed at how, at the worst possible moment, a point when they had given up hope of getting the bone fragment, it seemed to pop up. It was a...well, a miracle.

"Nancy, Sarah is going to be all right," he finally said and watched as she sagged against him with relief.

Bursting into tears again, she said, "W…what took so long?"

"It was a very hard surgery. The bone fragment had worked its way down farther than the pictures showed. One wrong move could have been very dangerous. We didn't think we were going to be able to remove it. Then just a little while ago, just as we were about to give up, the bone fragment seemed to almost appear right in front of our forceps. It was a miracle, Nancy. I felt the peace of God come into that surgery room. I knew he was there."

Nancy smiled a sweet wondering smile, still with tears falling down her cheeks. She haltingly told Marc what she had been praying, just a little while ago. "I know it was God—it had to be. It was seven o'clock when I came in here and started praying."

Marc looked at her incredulously. "I glanced at the clock on the surgery wall at seven and started asking for God's help."

Nancy felt Marc's arms go around her and hold her tight. She felt the peace and the comfort that he gave, and she knew that God was smiling down on them, and that Sarah was going to be fine.

Chapter 26

Nancy watched with joy as Sarah was adjusting the crown of fall flowers that were encircling her head. "Mommy, is my bald spot showing?"

"No, honey, you're beautiful," Nancy said as she lifted up her candlelight wedding dress and moved toward her daughter.

Mrs. Montgomery spoke up, "If you ask me, I think you're both beautiful."

Susan, Nancy's maid of honor, spoke up, "I'll add an extra amen to that one!"

Several other voices chimed in, all of them the bridesmaids that were helping Nancy get ready to walk down the aisle to Marc. Nancy turned and smiled at them all. She was amazed that she had gotten to know so many people in the few months between Sarah's miraculous recovery until now. There was no other way to explain it. It was just God blessing her abundantly, and she knew it.

She thought about the man who was about to become her husband. Her heart raced to think of how handsome he was, and that he would be waiting at the front of the church for her to make her entrance…as she was going to become his wife.

When she had married Joe, they had only went to Vegas and gotten married. Joe hadn't wanted a big show, he said it would cost too much money, and she had agreed. But so often she had longed for a traditional wedding…and now all of it was coming true. She felt like she was living in a fairy tale.

A voice behind her spoke up, "My dear, you are absolutely lovely, and I hope my nephew realizes what a jewel he's getting."

Nancy, recognizing the voice, turned and smiled. "Aunt Nettie, I'm the one that getting the best bargain."

"Harrumph, that's what you think. That nephew of mine can be pretty stubborn sometimes, but I love him. And I know that you'll be the perfect wife for him. Nancy, I am so happy that Marc decided to let God show him he could love again." Aunt Nettie dabbed a linen hanky at one corner of her eye.

Nancy felt tears forming in her eyes also when she thought about how God had also taught her how to love and be loved. "Aunt Nettie, God has given us both a miracle. It seemed as if everything we lost, he gave us back a thousand times over."

"God is like that, Mommy," Sarah chimed in. "I know 'cause I asked Dr. Angel if he would watch over you if something happened to me when I got operated on. But you know what? While Dr. Angel was operating on my head, God told me that I would get to be with you today. So I knew it was okay. God is really good, huh, Mommy?"

Kneeling down and pulling Sarah into her arms, she said, "Yes, darling, God is really good."

Aunt Nettie spoke up, "Oh my, I need to get out there. I hear the music starting, and I want to see my precious new great niece walk down that aisle with her beautiful princess dress on." She leaned down and kissed Sarah on her cheek. "I'll be watching for you, and I'll take your picture, so smile real big."

"Okay, Auntie Nettie, I will," Sarah replied with a gap-tooth grin...she had lost her first tooth just before the wedding.

Hurrying Nancy, Susan, and Sarah toward the front of the room, Mrs. Montgomery kissed her two daughters and her granddaughter. "Now Nettie Matthews said it just right...I want all of you to smile big!"

They all laughed as she left the room to be escorted down the aisle to sit in her place of honor as the mother of the bride.

Susan took a deep breath and said, "Well, sis, are you ready to become Mrs. Marc Carter?"

"More than you will ever know," Nancy replied.

"Does that make me Sarah Carter...or would I be called Sarah Angel?" Sarah chirped up.

"I think Dr. Angel is going to want to change your name," Nancy said because she and Marc had already talked it over. He wanted to adopt Sarah and change her name as soon as possible.

"Goody, 'cause I really like the name angel." Sarah inserted.

"Ah...Sarah...about your name for Marc, do you think you could change it some?" Nancy had wanted to approach Sarah now about calling Marc Dad or something different than Dr. Angel.

"But why, Mommy?" Sarah asked bewildered.

"Well...because..." Nancy didn't get to finish because the time had come for Susan to walk down the aisle.

Susan grinned and winked at both Nancy and Sarah and then walked down the aisle to stand in her place.

"It's your turn, princess," Nancy whispered and watched with pride as her daughter walked slowly down the white strip of carpet, stopping every few feet to drop some rose petals. When she would stop to drop the rose petals, she would look at whoever was in the pew where she stopped, and she would say, "I'm getting a new daddy today!"

Laughter and tears filled the entire church as they watched the little girl finish dropping all of the petals out of her basket at the bottom of the stairs. Suddenly she looked up and saw Marc standing there with a smile on his face.

Grinning, she said, "Hi, Daddy Angel!"

"Hi, princess!" Marc said with a gravelly voice full of emotion.

How good God had been to him to give him another beautiful, precious little girl to love and protect. Then he heard the wedding march and looked up.

Make that two beautiful, precious girls to protect, he thought. But when he caught his first glimpse of Nancy, everything blanked out of his mind but the beautiful woman that was gracefully walking toward him.

They had decided that since Nancy's father was gone, she would just walk down the aisle by herself because she was giving her whole life to him. He couldn't take his eyes off her as she came toward him.

Stopping in front of the church, Nancy's eyes never left Marc's the whole time she walked toward him. Here was her groom, and she was his bride. From this moment on, they would be a family, a forever family that would love and cherish each other, one that would trust God to help them through the hard times. After all, that's what a family was all about!

About the Author

Brenda Davis is a small business owner, entrepreneur, and homemaker. Her greatest accomplishment is keeping up with her two granddaughters. She has been a Christian since she was twelve years old. She enjoys working in her garden, cooking for her family, keeping her grandchildren, and of course, reading and writing. She writes short stories, along with Western books and even a teen Christian book.

God had always been foremost in her and her husband's life. Her husband, Alvin, has pastored two different churches, and although they are not pastoring now, their life is full with their small business, kids, and grandchildren.

CPSIA information can be obtained
at www.ICGtesting.com
Printed in the USA
BVHW080948150323
660486BV00004B/138